*Here is a complete list of exciting
Happy Hollister books you
should read:*

The Happy Hollisters at Lizard Cove

By Jerry West

Illustrated by Helen S. Hamilton

DOUBLEDAY & COMPANY, INC.

GARDEN CITY, N. Y.

Contents

CHAPTER 1

A TINY TRAVELER

"PAM, wait for me!" Holly Hollister called to her sister. She bent her head into the blustery February sleet storm as she ran down the school walk.

"I will," Pam replied, then giggled. "Hurry, or your pigtails may freeze straight out before we get home."

Hand in hand the sisters trotted along until they caught up with their two brothers, Pete and Rickey. Together the children ran the rest of the way. Pete, twelve, was the oldest, with Pam next. She was ten, Ricky seven, and Holly six.

As they neared their home on Shoreham Road, Rickey cried out, "Look! There's an express truck in our driveway. A man's carrying in a crate."

Eager to find out what was inside it, the children doubled their speed.

"Do you live here?" the expressman asked, as they reached him.

"Yes," Pete replied.

"Then these are your pineapples," the man said.

5

"Pineapples!" the children chorused in surprise. "Who sent them?"

"That's a mystery," the driver replied with a wink. "They came all the way from Puerto Rico, but there's no sender's name or address on the crate."

"That's funny," said Pete.

The truckman lifted the crate to his shoulder and the children followed him to the kitchen door of their large, rambling house, which was on the shore of Pine Lake. Pete opened the door and asked the man to set the crate on a table. He signed the delivery book and the driver went off.

Just then little Sue Hollister, a vivacious four-year-old, ran into the room. Her eyes grew wide as saucers. "Oh, Mother," she cried out, "come and see our s'prise!"

As the other children kicked off their boots and removed their coats, Mrs. Hollister, a slender, blond-haired woman, hurried into the kitchen. She looked first at the crate, then at the children. Pete, tall, good-looking and wearing a crew cut, was grinning broadly. Blond, pretty Pam had tiny dimples which now showed plainly. Ricky, who had red hair and freckles, was peering through the slats of the crate.

"Do you know anyone in Puerto Rico, Mother?" Pam asked.

"No."

"Does Dad?"

"No. Why?"

"Then we have a mystery to solve," Pete said excitedly.

"A pineapply mystery," Holly added.

Mrs. Hollister smiled as she inspected the label on the crate. "The fruit is for us all right, and from San Juan in Puerto Rico."

"Let's open the crate," Ricky urged.

Pete got a claw hammer and tore the strips of wood from the top.

"What luscious looking pineapples!" Mrs. Hollister said as she lifted one out.

"Four, eight, twelve, sixteen," Holly counted. "There are sixteen of them!"

"Where is Rico-Rico?" Sue asked, cocking her head inquisitively.

As the others giggled, Pam ran to get her geography book and found the map of the Caribbean islands.

"It's right here." She showed Sue, pointing out the second island east of Cuba. "San Juan is the capital. It's about two thousand miles from here."

"Yikes!" Ricky exclaimed. "The pineapples came a long way!"

At their mother's suggestion the children carried the fruit into the pantry and put it on a shelf. As Holly set one of the golden pineapples down, she jumped back and shrieked.

"Oooh, look!"

In the crown of the pineapple lay a tiny lizard!

7

"Oooh look!"

The little creature, about six inches long, was very still. Everyone crowded around.

"How did he get in here, Mother?" Holly asked.

Mrs. Hollister said she supposed the lizard had crawled into the crate in Puerto Rico and had come all the way to the U.S. by boat.

"Is he dead?" Ricky asked.

"I hope not," said kindhearted Pam.

Tears came to Sue's eyes. "Maybe the poor little lizard got frozen," she wailed.

Pete lifted him gently from the top of the pineapple and said the reptile was still breathing. He put him on a chair near the kitchen radiator. Ricky dropped to his knees, intently studying the strange visitor.

Pam, meanwhile, hurried into the living room for a book on reptiles. She returned, reading it.

"What are you looking up?" Holly asked her.

Pam said she wanted to find out whether the lizard might be poisonous. After reading a few minutes, she shook her head. "The only poisonous ones are the Gila monster found in the American Southwest and the Mexican beaded lizard," she reported.

Sue dried her tears and said, "This lizard isn't wearing beads. He's all right."

"Oh, Sue, you're a case," Pam told her with a chuckle.

Suddenly Ricky shouted, "Look! The lizard's moving!"

The heat had had its effect and the tiny traveler began to stir his stubby legs.

"Quick! Let's find a bed for him!" Holly said excitedly. She ran down the cellar steps to locate something in which to put him.

Pam continued to read about lizards. The one in front of her apparently was an iguana, whose home is the Caribbean islands. "The article says they're friendly and playful," Pam said. "May we keep this one for a pet, Mother?"

"Of course, dear."

Holly soon returned with a large plastic beach pail which she had used the summer before. A little sand was still left in the bottom of it. "Shall I pour the sand out?" she asked.

"Oh no," said Pam. "Lizards like sand."

"But I think you ought to add a bed of paper shreds so the lizard can keep warm," Mrs. Hollister suggested.

In a few minutes the children had cut up a sheet of newspaper into small bits and put them on top of the sand. Then the lizard was put into his new home.

"He likes it! He's blinking his eyes," Sue said, jumping up and down with excitement.

"What shall we call him?" Holly asked.

"How about Lucky?" Pam suggested. "He certainly was lucky to survive the trip all the way from Puerto Rico."

The others agreed this was a good name and they

all watched closely as Lucky became more and more frisky.

"May I pick him up?" Sue asked wistfully.

Mrs. Hollister said she might if she were careful. Sue gently lifted the lizard and set him on the back of her hand. Lucky blinked his beady eyes and looked about, then began to climb up Sue's arm. She giggled so hard that Lucky nearly fell off.

Each child took a turn playing with the new pet. Then, as Pam put Lucky back in the sand pail, the children heard the family station wagon come into the driveway.

"Daddy's home!" Holly exclaimed and hurried to open the back door for him.

Mr. Hollister was a tall, athletic man with a jolly smile. The minute he stepped inside the house Sue jumped into his arms and gave him a hug. Then, holding her daddy's hands tightly, the little girl did an upside-down flip-flop and landed feet first on the floor.

After Holly had kissed her father she exclaimed, "Daddy, come see our lizard! His name's Lucky!"

Mr. Hollister admired the new pet, then asked where the children had bought it.

"Lucky came free," said Holly and showed her father the pineapples.

Sue crowded in. "Daddy, do you have a lizard friend in Rico-Rico?" she asked.

Mr. Hollister chuckled and said he knew no one who lived on the Caribbean island.

11

"I'll phone the express office and see if it has a record of the sender," he offered. But the clerk in charge said the bill of lading did not state this.

"So we have a very kind, unknown friend," Mr. Hollister declared.

Pete had gone to the kitchen door in answer to a whine and a bark outside. When he opened it the Hollisters' collie Zip bounded in.

"Take it easy," Pete warned.

"Yes," said Holly. "Don't you hurt our new lizard!"

Pete led Zip to the sand pail and let the dog sniff and gaze. Then he patted him. "It's okay, old fellow. That lizard has a right to be here."

Satisfied, Zip trotted off. He went at once to his feed bowl and waited until Pam put food into it.

While the Hollisters were eating their supper a little later, Pam remarked how nice it would be to visit Puerto Rico.

Holly agreed. "Or any place where it's hot," she said, looking up from her dessert of baked custard. "I'd like to go swimming!"

"Me too!" Ricky added. "Or paddle a canoe!"

"I want to visit the South Pole, Sue piped up. "That's the southest hottest place of all."

The others laughed and Mr. Hollister explained to Sue that the South Pole was covered with ice and snow, the same as the North Pole.

"Then they gave it the wrong name," Sue remarked. "It should be North Pole Number 2."

12

"I wonder," said Pam, "how Lucky will like it up north." Then she asked, "May we take him to school tomorrow, Mother?"

Mrs. Hollister said they might if they would keep the lizard warm and not expose him to the wintry weather.

"Goody," said Holly.

Before going to bed Pete put a piece of wire screen over the sand pail and left it near the kitchen radiator. Seeing this, Zip curled up beside the pail as if to guard the lizard.

"Good night," Pete said, patting the dog.

In the morning the lizard was livelier than ever. He looked up from the bottom of the pail and blinked.

"Lucky's hungry," Holly said.

"I know what we can give him," Ricky exclaimed.

"What?"

"Turtle food. I have some in a box left from last July." Ricky had captured two snapping turtles near the dock the summer before and had kept them until fall.

The boy hastened to a shelf in the kitchen and returned with a small box half full of dried insects. He sprinkled several in front of Lucky's nose. The lizard ate them hungrily.

"And now for your own breakfasts," Mrs. Hollister said, spooning hot cereal into bowls. The children took their places at the dining-room table.

After breakfast Pam got an oblong, cardboard

13

jewel box from her dresser. A strip of soft cotton lay in the bottom of it. She punched several holes in the lid, then placed Lucky in the box and put an elastic band around it.

"I'll hold Lucky under my coat to keep him warm," the girl promised as she kissed her mother good-by.

The sleet storm had ended, leaving the streets of Shoreham covered with a slick coating of ice. Pam walked mincingly, holding the little box snugly under her coat. When she and her sister and brothers caught up with several schoolmates, the Hollisters told them about Lucky.

"You mean you really have a live lizard?" asked Ann Hunter, a curly-haired girl of Pam's age, who lived down the street.

"May we see it?" begged her blue-eyed brother Jeff. He was eight.

"When we get to school, I'll show him to all of you," Pam promised.

The moment the doors opened she hurried inside, her friends following. They hung up their coats in the lockers, then returned to the main hall. Pam opened Lucky's box. She had five minutes in which to exhibit the pet before the starting bell would sound.

"Oh, he's cute!" exclaimed Ann. Pam let her hold Lucky, and the lizard swished its tail back and forth like a happy puppy.

"It looks like a tiny dinosaur," remarked Dave

14

Mead, a dark-haired friend of Pete's who had studied about prehistoric animals.

After several other pupils had seen the lizard and left for their classrooms, Joey Brill walked down the corridor. Joey was Pete's age, but a larger boy. Ever since the Hollisters had moved to Shoreham, Joey had bothered them with underhanded tricks.

Seeing Pam fasten the lid of the box, he asked, "Hey, what you got in there?"

"A lizard."

"Let me see him."

Pam removed the lid again and waited for him.

"Oh, a snake with legs," said Joey wisely.

"He does belong to the reptile family," Pam agreed.

"Ugh!" Joey remarked. "Reptiles are no good."

"They are too," said Pam. "They're a big help to farmers. They eat insects."

She wished Joey would hurry, because she did not want to be late for class. Besides, Pam sensed he might try some kind of trick.

"I wish Pete were here," she thought. Her brother always protected her.

Suddenly Joey snatched the box and started down the hall.

Pam gasped. "Come back! Give me my lizard!" But Joey ran on.

Pam chased him down the hall past Pete's room. Suddenly the bell rang.

"Please, Joey! We'll both be late," she begged.

15

The girl finally trapped Joey at the end of the hall. But he was determined not to be caught.

"Try and get me!" he cried. He opened a door to the schoolyard and dashed from the building.

"Come back!" Pam cried frantically. "Lucky will freeze!"

CHAPTER 2

MRS. VANILLA

"Joey!" Pam cried, hurrying after him into the icey schoolyard. "You can't take Lucky. Bring him back!"

The bully turned and held the box toward her. But when Pam reached for it, Joey teasingly snatched it away. He kept dodging back and forth just out of her reach.

Suddenly the school door was flung open and Pete Hollister ran out. From his classroom he had heard his sister's call and hurried outside to help her. Pete dashed after Joey and caught him by his shirt collar.

"*Gulp!*" Joey said, skidding to a stop.

"Give Pam the lizard," Pete ordered sternly.

"Okay, okay. Take him!" Joey sulked.

He tossed the box toward the girl. It turned upside down and the lizard flew out!

"Oh!" Pam exclaimed.

She moved quickly and fortunately caught Lucky in her hands. Holding the little pet close to her, she hurried inside the building.

Pete bent down to pick up the empty box. As he did, Joey gave him a hard thump on the back.

"Ow!" Pete groaned, the breath nearly knocked out of him.

"That's what you get for butting in," Joey said, sneering. "Serves you right !"

Pete was angry. He whirled about and hit Joey on the nose. The bully cried out and danced around in pain, finally running indoors again. Pete followed close behind. He found Pam waiting in the corridor and gave her the box.

"Thanks, Pete," she said. "You saved poor Lucky's life."

"You mean you did by catching him," her brother stated with a grin.

Pam put the lizard into the box and hurried off to her class. Pete caught up to Joey who was just entering their room. The other pupils snickered when they saw Joey holding a hand over his red nose.

"I'll get you for this," Joey muttered to Pete as they took their seats.

In Pam's classroom meanwhile, the children had gathered about Lucky. Miss Nelson, their teacher, explained that the iguana of the Caribbean is small, but a variety in tropical and Central America grows large, often as long as six feet.

"It is pale greenish-gray in color," she explained. "And sometimes marked with black. Around its tail are several broad, black rings."

"Oooh, I'm glad Pam's iguana is a tiny one," exclaimed a girl named Helen Pierce.

Pete whirled about and hit Joey back.

The lizard was put back in its box and not disturbed for the rest of the school day. When the last bell rang, Pam went for the pet. She met Pete outside and the two hurried to join Ricky and Holly. On the way home Pete told the others of the threat Joey had made.

Ricky gave a grunt of disgust. "Joey can't scare me!"

"Just the same, we'd better watch out for him," Pam advised.

The Hollisters kept a sharp lookout for Joey or his friend, Will Wilson, who sometimes joined Joey in his annoying tricks. But neither boy showed up.

Turning into Shoreham Road, Pam said, "I wonder if Mother knows yet who sent the pineapples."

"And Lucky," Holly added.

They hurried inside the house. Mrs. Hollister was in the kitchen cutting up two of the pineapples for dessert. When questioned by Pete, she said:

"No, I haven't found out. I thought a letter of explanation might come."

She handed each of the children a luscious slice of pineapple.

"Yummy! It's super," Ricky said, and reached for another piece.

"That's all until mealtime," his mother said.

At this moment the telephone rang. Pete went into the hall to answer. A man at the express office was calling to say he had just found a record on the shipper of the fruit.

"What was that name?" Pete asked, not understanding the man. The clerk spelled the name and Pete scribbled it on a piece of paper. He said thank you and hung up.

"Guess what," he said, returning to his family. "Our pineapples were sent from San Juan by a Mrs. Villamil."

The children looked at their mother. "Do you know her?" Holly asked.

Mrs. Hollister thought a moment, then replied she did not remember anyone with that name.

"Perhaps Mrs. Villamil is someone you knew a long time ago," Pam guessed, "but you don't know her married name."

Mrs. Hollister said this might be true. She would write Mrs. Villamil anyway and ask if the pineapples had been intended for the Hollisters.

That evening at dinner, while the family was eating the tempting pineapple dessert, the telephone rang again. Sue, who was nearest the hall, jumped up.

After lifting the receiver and saying hello, the little girl's face took on an excited expression. Holding a chubby hand over the mouthpiece, she called, "Mother, it's Mrs. V-V-Vanilla!"

For a moment the family looked at one another in amazement. Then Mrs. Hollister smiled. "You mean Mrs. Villamil?"

21

Sue bobbed her head as her mother hurried to the telephone. Everyone listened curiously as Mrs. Hollister talked. Then as soon as she finished speaking, questions flew from her family's lips.

"Who is she?"

"Did she send the pineapples?"

"Do you know her, Mother?"

"What did she say?"

Mrs. Hollister laughingly told her family that Mrs. Villamil's maiden name was Grace Elkins and she was a girlhood friend. She had married Dr. Villamil of Puerto Rico and now lived near San Juan. They had two children, Maya, eleven, and Carlos, twelve. The Hollisters' Uncle Russ had met the family while on a business trip and had given them the Hollisters' Shoreham address.

"Is Mrs. Villamil in Shoreham now?" Pam asked.

"No, she's in New York, looking up schools for her children to attend next year. Maya and Carlos are with her. I invited them to visit us."

"And will they?" Pam asked eagerly.

"Yes. They'll fly here tomorrow afternoon if the weather permits and will leave Friday morning."

"Goody!" cried Holly. "Wednesday to Friday."

After supper Pam and Holly helped their mother tidy the guest room for Mrs. Villamil and Maya. Carlos would bunk with Ricky.

With preparations ready, the children studied their homework, then started for bed. Ricky fed Lucky and put clean shredded papers in his pail. Then he asked if he might take Lucky to his and Pete's room overnight.

"I'll put him on the table between our beds," the boy said.

Mrs. Hollister thought it might be too cold and suggested that he leave the sand pail on the table in the second-floor hall.

Pam giggled. "We wouldn't dare leave Lucky near Rick's arms. He might knock the lizard over." All the Hollisters knew that sometimes Ricky dreamed he was a cowboy lassoing horses and flung his arms about.

Ricky made a face at his sister, then carried the sand pail upstairs. He put the little screen on top of the lizard's bed and left it on the hall table.

When Ricky awakened next morning, the first thing he did was go to look in the pail. He blinked his sleepy eyes, then rubbed them with the back of his hands.

"Yikes!" he exclaimed. "What happened?"

The little screen lid lay on the table and the pail was empty. Lucky had disappeared!

Ricky quickly spread the alarm and everybody joined in a search for the lizard. The hall and each bedroom was thoroughly combed. No Lucky.

"Where could he have gone?" Ricky asked, feeling responsible.

"Maybe he's downstairs," Pam suggested.

The children hurried to the first floor and even

got Zip to help in the search. None of them could find Lucky.

The hunt was delayed temporarily while the family ate breakfast, but Ricky hardly touched the meal. Afterward, as the children made their own beds, every sheet and blanket was carefully examined. But Lucky could not be found.

"Hurry, or you'll be late for school," Mrs. Hollister warned.

Pete, Pam, Ricky, and Holly reluctantly donned their hats and coats.

"Don't worry," Mrs. Hollister added, trying to brighten their sad expressions. "I'll search until I find Lucky."

"Oh dear, I hope he's not hurt," Holly said as she went to pick up her half-opened pencil box from the desk in the living room. She looked in it and squealed.

"*Lucky!*"

The lizard was snuggling in an empty space between a red eraser and a blue pencil. How relieved everybody was!

Ricky laughed. "Lucky wants to go to school again!"

Mrs. Hollister felt it would be best, however to leave the pet at the house where it was warm. "And hurry home immediately after school," she said. "We'll all go to the airport to meet the Villamils."

At three o'clock that afternoon they were eagerly awaiting the arrival of Mr. Hollister from The

24

Trading Post. This was a combination hardware and sports store he operated in the business section of Shoreham.

"Here he comes!" Sue called, peeking out of a front window.

She hurried to open the door and everyone went to the station wagon. As they drove to the airport, Pete glanced up at the dark sky with a concerned look.

"I wonder how the flying weather from New York is," he said.

Sue, who was riding in front between her mother and father, turned on the radio. To their disappointment, the local announcer said that a snowstorm was on its way. A couple of minutes later a few flakes began to fall. By the time the Hollisters reached the airport the snow was coming down hard.

"Oh, I do hope the Villamils can land here," Pam said as the family entered the airport building.

The plane was due at half past three, but by three forty-five it had not yet arrived. Ten minutes later Sue glanced up at a large clock.

"Oh dear," she sighed. "It's one inch to four already."

Her funny expression eased the Hollisters' concern for a moment. Then Pete hurried over to the information desk.

"Flight 47 is on its way," the woman clerk told him, smiling. "There's nothing to worry about."

Pete returned with the news, but still the plane

did not arrive. Minutes ticked away. Then suddenly Holly shouted, "I hear it!"

The Hollisters scanned the leaden sky and spotted a big silver-winged airplane coming down. It landed at the far end of the field and taxied up in front of the main building. Despite the storm the family hurried out to the gate.

"Mother," said Pam, "do you suppose Mrs. Villamil has changed much since you knew her long ago?"

Mrs. Hollister said that her friend had been a very pretty girl and probably was the same today. As several women walked down the steps from the plane, Mrs. Hollister looked intently but did not recognize any of them.

Presently, however, she smiled. "I see Grace—the one in the brown coat!"

A lovely-looking, dark-haired woman with a slender figure alighted from the plane, followed by two sun-tanned children. The Hollisters ran through the gate to greet them.

"Grace, it's so good to see you!" Mrs. Hollister said happily, giving her friend a quick hug.

"Elaine, you haven't changed a bit!" Mrs. Villamil responded with a charming smile.

"And neither have you!"

Introductions were quickly made. The Hollister children immediately liked their guests. Maya had black hair and large brown eyes. A dimple appeared in her right cheek when she smiled. Carlos looked much like his sister but he was taller.

Both children spoke perfect English with a delightful Spanish accent. They teased the northerners about greeting them with a snowstorm.

"You can show me how to make snowballs," Carlos said, "and we will play soldier."

The young people linked arms and, chatting gaily, hurried to the station wagon. As soon as the baggage was brought, Mr. Hollister drove off.

"To think you're the ones who sent us the pineapples," he said, chuckling. "Thanks so much. We're enjoying them tremendously."

"That was just our greeting card," Mrs. Villamil said with a musical little laugh. "We grow thousands of pineapples on our island."

Holly told the Villamils about finding a lizard in one of the pineapples. The Puerto Ricans were amazed that Lucky had survived the long trip in winter.

Carlos said, "Maya and I have lots of lizards to play with. It's fun!"

"But what interests my children right now," Mrs. Villamil said, "is the snow. This is the first time they have seen any."

"We've had too much of it this year," Pam said. "We're looking forward to summer."

"But it's lovely!" Maya protested. "As light and fluffy as cotton."

She asked if she might open the window alongside her and put her hand out to feel the snowflakes.

"Certainly," Mrs. Hollister said.

As Maya reached out, Pete suddenly gave a warning shout. A snowball was whizzing toward the car. It flew through the window Maya had opened and hit her hard on the neck.

"Oh-h!" she cried out.

CHAPTER 3

A SLIDING CHAMPION

WHEN the snowball hit Maya Mr. Hollister stopped the car and backed up to look for the thrower.

"Someone's ducking down that alley!" Pete shouted as he caught a glimpse of a boy disappearing into a back yard. But it was snowing so hard the runner could not be identified.

"I'll bet he was Joey Brill," Ricky said hotly. "Who else would do a thing like that?"

"It might have been Will Wilson," Holly guessed. "He lives near here."

Mr. Hollister apologized to the Villamils for the unpleasant incident. Meanwhile, his wife and Pam wiped the snow from Maya's neck. Fortunately the little girl had not been hurt and the station wagon went on. Shortly afterward it pulled into the Hollisters' driveway.

"What a lovely home you have," Mrs. Villamil said, as the boys carried the luggage inside.

"It must be fun having a lake up to your back lawn," added Maya.

"It is," Pam said. "Boating and swimming in summer and skating in the winter."

The visitors were shown to their rooms. From the boys' room Carlos could look over the wide expanse of Pine Lake, which was a mass of solid ice.

"*Es splendido!*" he said.

Next the guests were introduced by Holly to Zip. The friendly collie nudged them with his nose and licked their hands.

"He's fun to play with in the snow," Holly said. She added, "Come, I'll show you our kittens."

She led Maya and Carlos to the basement where White Nose and her five kittens nestled in a large cardboard box. Maya chuckled as Holly told her their names: Midnight, Snowball, Tutti-Frutti, Smokey and Cuddly.

"What cute names!" the dark-eyed girl exclaimed.

"Where's your lizard?" Carlos asked.

"In the kitchen."

They all ran up to pay a call on Lucky in his sand pail. The Villamil children said Lucky was indeed a real iguana.

Maya now told the Hollisters that her family lived a few miles east of San Juan in a place called Lizard Cove.

"Do lizards live there too?" Ricky asked.

"Yes, lots of them," Maya replied.

"You'd like it there," Carlos added. "On one corner of our property is an old stone tower."

"Is it spooky?" Ricky asked.

"Sort of. We think it was built by the early explorers, maybe even Christopher Columbus. He discovered Puerto Rico, you know."

"On his second trip to North America," Maya added. "And Ponce de Leon was the first governor."

The children exchanged stories all through the evening. Occasionally Carlos and Maya would go to a window and look out at the deepening snow.

"I want to walk in it," Maya said.

"Sure, tomorrow morning," Pete said, smiling. "We'll take you to our school if you'd like to go."

"*Bueno!*" Carlos said.

Holly looked puzzled and Maya chuckled. "He said 'good,' " the girl explained. "You'll have to learn some of our Spanish expressions." Maya told them that English was spoken in Puerto Rico, but the native people used Spanish most of the time.

"And now, *buenas noches,*" said Mrs. Villamil "Good night. I think my children and I should go to bed."

Next morning Pete lent Carlos a pair of his boots and Pam offered extra ones of hers to Maya.

"Come on, Carlos!" Pete said, shortly before the others were ready to go to school. "Let's clear the porch and the sidewalk."

The two boys hurried for brooms and shovels, and by the time the rest of the children were ready to leave the house the snow had been cleared from the steps and a neat path made to the sidewalk.

"You'll have to step high," Pam warned.

31

Carlos took a spill!

Lifting their feet, the six children plowed through the drifts, but finally arrived at Lincoln School.

Mr. Logan, the janitor, had already cleared the walks. In one place near the playground, however, some boys and girls had sprinkled snow on the sidewalk and were making a slippery slide. Carlos and Maya looked on in amazement as the pupils ran fast, then glided over the stretch of slippery walk.

"That's a great game!" Carlos said. "I'd like to try it."

"Go ahead," Pete urged.

But alas! Carlos had hardly started on the slide when he lost his balance and took a spill!

"I guess I'll have to practice," he said, picking himself up.

The school bell rang and everyone hurried inside. Ricky and Holly went directly to their rooms, but Pete and Pam led their guests to the principal's office and introduced Carlos and Maya to Mr. Russell.

"I'm very glad to meet you," he said, "and I hope you will enjoy your visit to our school."

After chatting with Maya and Carlos a few minutes Mr. Russell asked them if they danced.

The visitors modestly admitted that they could. "Carlos and I have learned one Spanish dance which we do together," Maya said, dimpling.

"Would you perform it at assembly this morning?" Mr. Russell asked.

"Si, yes," Carlos spoke up. "With pleasure!"

The Villamil children remained with Mr. Russell

while Pete and Pam went to their classes. When the assembly bell rang everybody trouped into the auditorium.

After the salute to the flag and the singing of the Star Spangled Banner, Mr. Russell held the rest of the morning exercises. Then he said:

"I have a surprise for all of you this morning. Friends of the Hollisters from Puerto Rico are visiting them and have consented to do a Spanish dance for us."

He introduced Carlos and Maya. Nearly everyone smiled and clapped but above the applause could be heard a loud boo. It came from the direction of Joey Brill, who was slumped low in his seat near the rear of the auditorium.

Mr. Russell looked at the boy sternly and Joey knew immediately the principal would tolerate no more rudeness. But the bully nudged Will Wilson, who was sitting next to him.

"The Hollisters think they're so smart bringing their friends to school. Those Puerto Ricans don't look like Americans."

This remark was overheard by Dave Mead, Pete's best friend. He leaned over in his seat behind Joey and said:

"Well, they're just as much Americans as we are. Don't you know that Puerto Rico is part of the United States?"

Joey scowled and looked embarrassed as Carlos and Maya, accompanied by the school pianist, began their dance. Standing erect and tapping their heels, they went through several intricate steps. When they finished the pupils clapped loudly and gave three cheers.

When the assembly was over Maya joined Pam and Carlos went with Pete to their classrooms. Here they listened to the lessons until recess time.

"Let's go outside and play," Pete suggested to Carlos as the bell rang.

"May I try that slide game again?"

"Sure, come on!"

By the time Pete and Carlos reached the slippery sidewalk, Pam and Maya already were there talking with Holly and Ricky.

"They're going to have a contest!" Pam said. "Let's join in."

Several other pupils were taking practice slides. A moment later Joey Brill zipped past and slid a long way. On his way back, he shouted:

"Why don't the sissy dancers try it too?"

Carlos' dark eyes blazed but he did not retort. Instead he said quietly to Pete, "I'd like to beat that boy at this game. Teach me how to slide, Pete!"

"Okay. Watch this."

Pete showed Carlos how to make the running approach and take off with his right foot. On the first try Carlos slipped again and fell. Maya tried it and slipped too, as Joey and Will howled with laughter.

But the two Villamil children picked themselves

up and tried again. On the third effort they did well.

"The faster you run, the farther you'll slide," Pete explained as the contest was about to start.

All the children wishing to enter it lined up. Joey and Will shoved their way to the front of the line.

"Ha! You think you can beat us?" Joey called at Pete and Carlos.

One by one the children ran fast and whizzed over the ice. Will Wilson made a long slide, but Joey beat him by several inches. No one else did as well until Pete started across the slick surface. As he stopped the children shouted.

"Joey's mark is tied!"

Pam and Maya did well for the girls but did not come close to the boys' mark. Next came Carlos' turn. The Puerto Rican took a longer run than the other children. How fast he sped toward the icy strip! Then he put out his right foot and sailed over the ice.

"Look at him go!" Dave Mead shouted.

As Carlos slowed down, he passed Joey's mark by nearly a foot.

"Carlos wins!" Pam shouted gleefully.

"I want another try!" Joey scowled. "It wasn't fair. The ice is faster now."

He ran to the end of the walk and taking an even longer run than Carlos, he sped down the slide. But halfway along he teetered. Waving his arms wildly, Joey fell with a thud.

"Hurray, Carlos is the sliding champion!" Holly cried.

As the younger pupils began to use the slide Will grumbled to his pal, "Let's get back at them, Joey."

"How?"

"You'll see," Will said.

He edged toward the sliding strip. It was Ricky's turn. As the boy sailed along Will put out his foot and tripped him. Ricky sprawled flat.

"Oh, you meanie!" Pam cried out as she ran to help her brother up.

Joey roared with laughter and Will looked pleased, but not for long. Pete had seen Will's move and now gave him a hard shove, knocking Will down on his back. Then he straddled the bully, holding him tightly with a knee on either shoulder.

"Ricky!" Pete called. "Wash Will's face!"

The redhaired Hollister limped over with a handful of snow. Will cried out, squirmed and turned his head from side to side, but to no avail.

"There, take that!" Ricky said. "And don't ever trip me again."

"And don't throw snowballs at our car either!" Pete warned him.

"That wasn't me," Will said, puffing. "It was Joey!"

Hearing this Joey stepped forward as if to fight everybody. Carlos blocked his way. "Want to fight me?" he asked, but Joey backed away.

Pete let Will up just as the bell rang and everybody went back to their classrooms. The Villamils enjoyed school very much and were sorry when it was over. When they returned home that afternoon with Pete and Pam, Mrs. Hollister announced that she had arranged a little supper party for her young guests.

"Some of our children's friends are coming," she said.

Jeff and Ann Hunter were the first to arrive. They were followed by Donna Martin, a dimpled seven-year-old friend of Holly's, and Dave Mead. After supper the Hollisters played records and showed home movies. Then Mrs. Hollister gave each child a little favor wrapped in gayly colored paper.

As Maya unwrapped hers she cried out in delight. "A yo-yo! What fun!"

"I have one, too," Carlos exclaimed, and attached the string to the middle finger of his right hand.

"We all got them!" Ricky said.

Soon the Hollister living room was a blur of twirling yo-yos.

"This is one of the favorite sports in Puerto Rico," Maya said as she deftly twirled her toy back and forth. "It takes practice to be good."

Soon all eyes turned to Carlos. First he tossed his yo-yo into the air, then around his back. The others applauded his skillful performance.

"Show me how you do it, please," Holly cried.

"I will," Maya said kindly. "You hold it like this and you do this—" The yo-yo buzzed out along the string and back again.

"I'll try it now," Holly said eagerly.

She tossed the yo-yo away from her, but the string slipped from her finger. The toy flew across the room, straight for the clock on the mantel!

CHAPTER 4

A SNOWBALL SURPRISE

As THE yo-yo whizzed toward the beautiful clock, Holly screamed. In a flash Carlos leaped up and caught the toy with his left hand.

"Great catch!" Pete exclaimed. The others sighed in relief, for the clock was a family heirloom.

"Yikes! You must be a baseball player, Carlos!" Ricky declared admiringly. "That was terrific!"

"Yes—I do play a lot," the boy said, adding that nearly everybody on their island liked baseball.

"Most Puerto Rican boys are good ballplayers," Maya explained. "And the girls are too."

Shortly afterward the party ended and the guests went home. Maya helped Pam and Holly tidy the living room. When this was done Maya squeezed Pam's hand gently.

"Oh dear," she said, sighing. "To think we have to leave tomorrow. I've had such a wonderful time!"

"Can't you stay longer? Please do!"

Mrs. Villamil, overhearing the invitation, smiled. "We'd love to, dear, but we have already made flight reservations. Besides, I'm sure Dr. Villamil is becoming lonesome."

"I wish Carlos and Maya could stay with us," Ricky remarked. "We have winter vacation next week."

Mrs. Villamil's eyes lighted up. "Really? Well, that would be fun, but it gives me an idea. Suppose you Hollisters fly to San Juan and visit us!"

There was a moment of complete silence as the Hollisters looked at one another.

"Crickets! You mean it?" Pete blurted.

"Of course. We have a large home. There's room for all of you."

"Goody! Goody! When can we go?" Sue exclaimed, bouncing up and down like a rubber ball.

"Hurray!" Ricky grasped Holly's hands and the two children danced around.

There was such a babel of excited chatter that Mr. and Mrs. Hollister and Mrs. Villamil started to laugh.

"Goodness, Grace, that certainly is a generous offer," Mrs. Hollister said. "But entertaining a family as large as ours is a tremendous undertaking."

"We'd be delighted to do it," Mrs. Villamil said.

"Please come," Maya urged.

Mrs. Hollister could not conceal her own excitement. "What do you think, John?"

Mr. Hollister grinned boyishly. "Business has slowed down since Christmas," he said thoughtfully, "and the rush will not start again until next month. Perhaps this would be a good time for a vacation, Elaine."

42

"Good-by, good-by, see you soon!"

This time both Carlos and Maya joined in the cries of delight.

"It's all settled then," Mrs. Villamil said, giving Mrs. Hollister an affectionate hug. "Perhaps you can take the Sunday night plane from New York."

"We'll try," Mr. Hollister said.

"You'll arrive in San Juan early Monday morning," Mrs. Villamil said. "We'll be waiting for you at the airport."

The Hollister children had never been off the mainland. The prospect of flying two thousand miles over the ocean thrilled them so much that when they went to bed they could hardly fall asleep.

"But I'd better," Pam told herself, "if I want to wake up and go to the airport when Maya and Carlos leave." The plane for New York would leave at seven.

While the boys were dressing at six next morning, Pete mentioned the tower of rocks on the Villamil place in Puerto Rico. "Let's investigate it," he said.

"We'll do it," Carlos promised.

When breakfast was over and the luggage packed, the Hollisters drove their guests to the airport.

"How big is Puerto Rico?" Ricky asked.

"It's only a small island," Mrs. Villamil said. "One hundred miles wide by about forty miles from north to south. But it's full of unusual things to see."

She told about the great fields of sugar cane, the pineapple plantations and beautiful beaches.

"We must visit Luquillo beach," Maya said. "It's—it's—"

44

"Dreamy?" Pam asked, smiling.

"That's the word for it," Maya answered.

Puerto Rico sounded like a fairyland and the Hollisters' enthusiasm mounted by the minute. After many excited good-bys, the Villamils boarded the big plane and took off for their lovely homeland.

"Just think, Sunday we'll be doing this," Holly said excitedly.

Saturday morning was spent shopping for extra summer clothes. Mrs. Hollister bought sunsuits for Sue and dresses, shorts, and gay blouses for Pam and Holly. Pete and Ricky needed some slacks and bright-colored sports shirts, so next the family went to a boys' shop a few doors from The Trading Post.

A handsome young clerk with a black mustache waited on them. As Pete and Ricky selected cool summer shirts the clerk said, "You're going to Florida for your school holiday?"

"No," Ricky replied. "We're flying to Puerto Rico."

When he heard this, the clerk's eyes brightened. "Fine! A wonderful place! I have an uncle living there. Perhaps you could stop in and say hello for me."

"Glad to," Pete said. "How do we find him?"

"His name is Enrique Pino and he runs a music shop in Santurce, which is next to San Juan," the clerk went on.

Taking a card from his pocket, he jotted down the

45

name, remarking that his uncle Enrique's shop was on Avenida de Diego.

"And I'm Enrique Pino too," the clerk said. "I'm named for my uncle."

"If we get to Santurce, we'll stop in your uncle's shop," Pete promised, as the man wrapped their package.

As they left the clothing store the Hollisters saw Joey Brill standing on a mound of snow near the curb.

"He's been spying on us," Pete whispered to Pam. "I wonder why."

The bully waited until Mrs. Hollister had walked on with Sue and Holly. Then he ran up to the others. "I hope you all enjoy your trip," he said.

"Thank you, Joey," Pam said.

"I didn't mean to hurt your friends," Joey added. "And to prove it, Will and I would like to give you a going-away present."

The Hollisters felt uneasy over the strange offer. This did not sound like Joey!

"Where is the gift?" Ricky blurted, not seeing any package.

"Come on down the street. Will's keeping it for you," Joey said. He pointed to the next corner. "We'll be waiting for you there."

The Hollisters hesitated, sure some trick was going to be played on them. Finally Pete said, "I'll tell Mother not to wait for us."

As Joey hurried off, Pete went to tell Mrs. Hollister the three of them would come later.

Ricky, meanwhile, had said to Pam, "I'll see what Joey and Will are up to before we fall into a trap."

"All right, I'll wait here," Pam agreed.

Ricky circled around the block and returned a few minutes later out of breath.

"They're standing alongside that building with a big pile of snowballs," he reported to Pam and Pete.

"So that's their parting gift!" his brother exclaimed hotly. "An ambush!"

He clenched his fists. "I'd like to show them——"

"Let's have no more trouble," said Pam. We'll return home another way. Joey and Will can wait until next summer and all their snowballs will melt," she joked.

But Pete was not satisfied with this. He wanted to turn the tables—cause an ambush in reverse.

"Wait here a minute," he said, and ran down the side street his brother had taken. On the way he stopped to scoop up enough snow for two firm, round snowballs.

Cautiously he crept up to the building behind which Joey and Will were hiding. The bullies were peering toward the street, a snowball in each hand, waiting for the Hollisters to come by.

Standing in back of them, Pete had the advantage. Aiming precisely, he fired both snowballs in rapid succession. The first one struck Will's arm a glancing blow. The second clipped off Joey's cap. The bullies were so surprised that for a moment they stood open-mouthed in astonishment.

47

Pete ducked out of sight. Then, chuckling, he returned to his brother and sister and told what had happened. "They'll never know who hit them," he said.

"But they'll probably guess," Pam remarked.

"Serves Joey and Will right," said Ricky. "That was swell, Pete."

When the family gathered at the house a little later, Mrs. Hollister said the children's next chore was to take care of their pets. Dave Mead had volunteered to keep Zip at his house. Holly arranged that White Nose and her kittens would go to the Hunters' home.

"Who will take Lucky?" Sue asked.

Mrs. Hollister and the children discussed this for several minutes. Finally she suggested that they take Lucky back to his native land and let him go.

"I'm sure he'll be happier with his playmates," she said. "At least let's give him a chance."

The children disliked parting with the pet but agreed they did not want Lucky to be unhappy. If the little lizard should run away from them when they set him free and did not come back, then they would know this was what he wanted.

The following morning the family went to church. When they returned home, Tinker, a kind, elderly man who worked at The Trading Post, was waiting to drive the Hollisters to the airport.

"Have a swim for me," he told the children with a

grin as he bade the family good-by a little later. "And don't get into any trouble, children!"

They giggled and promised the kindly man, then went into the terminal building.

The baggage was checked and the excited family boarded the plane with Lucky.

Pam, Holly, and Sue had comfortable seats side by side. In front of them were Pete, Ricky, and Mrs. Hollister. Their father sat across the aisle.

A few minutes later the motors roared and the plane soared into the sky, heading for New York. Sue kept singing over and over:

"Hurray, hurray, we're on our way
To Rico-Rico! Watch us go!"

The other children giggled and peered eagerly out the window at the ground below until the plane was high above the clouds. Soon a pretty hostess brought trays with luncheon—lamb chops, creamed potatoes, fresh green peas, and ice cream and brownies.

"I like sky meals," Holly remarked, as she finished the last crumb.

When the big airplane landed in New York, the weather was cold and blustery. Though the Hollisters had a two-hour wait, they did not go outside the warm terminal building. Finally it was time for them to board the craft going to San Juan. As they climbed up the portable stairway into the fuselage, the airport blinked with red, green, and yellow lights.

"Isn't it beautiful!" Pam exclaimed as they took their seats.

"Will we be in lizard land soon?" Holly asked. She held Lucky's box in her lap. Then, taking off the lid, she stroked the creature's back.

"We're due early in the morning," Mrs. Hollister told her.

"Then Lucky and I'll go to sleep right away." She put the top on the box, tilted her seat back, and closed her eyes.

After the stewardess had made everyone comfortable, the big plane took off. The cabin lights were dimmed, pillows were supplied to passengers, and before long all the Hollister children were fast asleep.

The motion of the aircraft circling for a landing awakened them. Tilting their seats to an upright position they glanced out the window. It was dawn.

Below them lay an attractive airport ringed with swaying palms. Then trees with orange-colored flowers came into view and soon the tiny dots seen from above turned out to be people standing near the airport building. They were dressed in light clothes.

Sue could hardly believe what she saw. "Look, it's summer!" she exclaimed. "Wintertime never went so fast before!"

CHAPTER 5

STONE WRITING

THE huge airplane made a graceful turn, touched down lightly and taxied up in front of the large, white airport building.

Carrying their winter coats, the children stepped from the plane. As Pete walked down the steps, he cried out, "I see Carlos and Maya!"

The boy and girl were standing near their mother at the main gate. They waved to the Hollisters, then dashed to meet them.

"Hi!"

"Hi!"

"Welcome to San Juan!"

"Did you have a good flight?"

As the Hollisters reached Mrs. Villamil, Sue looked up at her. "I slept all the way from winter to summer —like a bear does!"

Mrs. Villamil laughed. "For that I'll give you a bear hug."

"Oh, it's wonderful here," Pam said, breathing in the sweet balmy air.

"We brought Lucky," said Holly, opening the lizard's box. Lucky lifted his head, blinked, and

51

looked about. "You're home again, sweetie," the girl cooed.

The little reptile replied by crawling up Holly's arm and tickling her neck with his nose.

Maya laughed. "I can't tell which he likes better —you or Puerto Rico."

Soon the two families were driving off in the Villamils' car, a roomy, cream and blue station wagon. Pretty flowers of all colors lined the roadway as they passed through quiet streets flanked by small pink and white bungalows.

"It's so different from where we live," Pam remarked, looking about.

She saw a street sign *Calle Maria* and asked what it meant. Maya said that *Calle* was the Spanish word for street. An avenue was called *avenida*.

A few minutes later Mrs. Villamil reached the ocean front and presently came to a little peninsula of pine trees and tall bamboo. She turned into it. Before them was a long driveway, at the end of which stood a beautiful one-story concrete house. It was a lovely shade of pink which blended with the green of the surrounding trees. Beyond it was the ocean.

"Welcome to Lizard Cove," said Mrs. Villamil as she stopped the car and everybody stepped out.

"Oh, look at the lizards!" Holly said, glancing around the ground. Little reptiles just like Lucky were scampering about the lawn.

Holly opened the box she carried and looked wist-

"Welcome to Puerto Rico."

fully at Lucky. "Do you want to be free?" she asked him.

"Wait!" Sue said. "We ought to dress Lucky up nice, so he'll look different from the other lizards."

While the Villamils smiled, the little girl reached into the pocket of her dress and pulled out a tiny piece of blue ribbon, which had been her doll's hair bow. Sue tied it gently to the lizard's tail while Holly held him.

"Now," Sue said as Holly put the lizard on the ground, "go play with your cousins."

At first the lizard did not move. "Shoo! Go on!" Ricky urged. The pet rubbed noses with another lizard, then scooted off under a large cactus bush.

"Oh dear," Holly said with a sigh, "I hate to see Lucky go, but I suppose he's happier now."

Just then a handsome man in a white suit drove in. As he stepped from the car, Mrs. Villamil took his hand and said proudly to the Hollisters:

"I'd like you to meet my husband, Dr. Villamil."

The doctor had black wavy hair, a neat mustache, and dancing brown eyes.

Bowing to Mrs. Hollister and shaking hands with her husband, he said, "We are so happy to have you visit us." He smiled at the Hollister children. "I hope you will have a great deal of fun. Right now you probably are very hungry as I am. A patient called me early so I have had no time to eat."

While they were waiting for breakfast, the children went to look at the ocean.

"Oh, how lovely!" exclaimed Pam a moment later as she gazed at the water.

Never before had the Hollisters seen anything more beautiful! Offshore the sea was emerald green, but closer to the beach there were patches of azure blue.

"What makes it change color?" Ricky asked.

Carlos explained that near the shore there were coral reefs just below the surface, which appeared to give the water a different hue.

Off to the right and a few feet in the surf loomed a large coral rock. The waves dashed against it, casting white spray in all directions.

The children returned to the house and Maya took her guests inside. The rooms were built around an open-air patio. Lush tropical plants grew in it with a delicately carved fountain in the center, spraying cool water into a basin below. Several gold fish swam about slowly in the water.

"Oh boy, you don't have to fish in the ocean," Ricky joked, as Maya showed the Hollisters to their quarters.

The large bedroom which Pam, Holly, and Sue were to share was painted a sea-green shade, with white furniture and gaily striped curtains. Pete's and Ricky's room had bright blue wallpaper decorated with sailing vessels.

Just then the children heard a tinkling bell. "Breakfast is ready," Maya said, leading them to the patio.

A large table was spread near the fountain and Mrs. Villamil assigned seats to her guests. On each plate was half of what the Hollister children thought was a melon. As they spooned out the luscious fruit, they noticed it had a sweet, mild flavor.

"Have you ever eaten papaya before?" Dr. Villamil asked them. When they said no, he added, "It's full of vitamins."

"Then you'd better eat lots of it, Ricky," said Holly. "It'll make your freckles fade."

This remark amused Dr. Villamil who said he had never heard this. Holly told him she had heard it lots of time.

As they were finishing bacon and eggs, which had been served by a pretty Puerto Rican maid, Pete asked, "Where's the mysterious rock tower you told me about, Carlos?"

"Up the beach a short distance. I'll show you."

An hour later the children put on their bathing suits and played in the water, with Mrs. Hollister and Mrs. Villamil watching them. Carlos and Maya were experts at diving through the waves and swimming with sure, strong strokes.

Pete and Pam kept up with them while Ricky, Holly, and Sue romped in the surf and splashed one another, swimming as best they could.

"I want to stay here forever!" cried Sue with delight, as she jumped the smaller waves with Holly.

When they had had enough swimming, Pete said

56

eagerly, "Let's look at the old monument now, Carlos."

"Okay." Carlos explained to his mother where they were going.

The seven children trudged westward along the beach, their feet sinking up to their ankles in soft sand. Soon they came to a strange-looking pile of rocks about twenty feet high. The mortar which had held them together was crumbling, making little toe holds one could use as steps.

"Come on! Let's look at the top of it," Pete suggested. "Maybe there's a mysterious message inside."

The Villamil children had never thought of this before but were eager to investigate. Excitedly Ricky told them that pirates often left messages in strange niches.

"They tell about buried treasure," he said. "This might be one of the places!"

Pete climbed to the top of the rock pile and stood up, getting a wonderful view of the ocean. Then he examined each stone without finding anything unusual. He climbed down and Pam went to try her luck. On first examination she could see nothing either.

"My turn next!" Ricky announced.

He scampered to the top of the rocks and felt each one carefully. The mortar, although worn thin, was still in place. There was one large, square shaped stone near the edge, however, which moved a little under his touch.

"Hey! This stone is loose!" Ricky called down. "Suppose we take it out and examine it."

"*Bueno*," said Carlos.

Ricky wriggled the stone back and forth, then yelled for a stick. Pete found a short piece of driftwood and, climbing part way up the rock pile, handed it to his brother. He used it as a wedge.

"The stone's moving!" he shouted.

Everyone stood back except little Sue. She had been dashing about picking up unusual pebbles and had not heard her brother's warning.

"Look out!" Ricky cried, as the stone toppled.

It headed directly toward Sue!

Maya grabbed Sue's arm and yanked her out of the way. The stone came tumbling down, missing the little girl by inches.

"Whew!" Pam exclaimed, as she thanked Maya. "That was almost an unlucky stone."

The large piece of rock had imbedded itself several inches in the sand. The boys pulled it out.

"Say, this is funny," Pete said. "There isn't any mortar on the stone."

He quickly climbed to the top of the pile and examined the spot where it had been wedged. There was no mortar on any of the stones on which the loose one had lain.

"Do you suppose the stone was meant to be taken out?" Carlos asked after Pete climbed down.

Pam thought so.

"Then you *have* run into a mystery here," Maya said excitedly.

"Let's take a good look at the stone," Pete suggested.

Turning it over, the children examined each of its sides carefully. The ends were smooth. The top was equally polished.

"But the bottom is rough," Pam observed, running the palm of her hand over it.

Carlos did the same. "Yes—there are little ridges," he remarked, and added that these might be printing.

Pam looked closely at the stone again. "You're right! Do you suppose it's a secret message?"

The Villamil children studied the printing carefully. Finally Carlos remarked, "It looks as if it's written in Spanish, but the outlines are so dim I can't make out most of the letters."

"Maybe Dad can help us," Maya said. "He's good at——" Her words were drowned out by the rackety sound of an aircraft nearby.

Glancing up, they saw a helicopter skimming above the water near the beach. The children raced out on the sand excitedly.

"Boy, it's low!" Ricky exclaimed.

The children could plainly see two men in it. One of them waved. Suddenly there was a sputtering sound and the helicopter's blades began to revolve more slowly.

"The engine's conked out," Pete cried.

The children looked on spellbound as the pilot fought to control the dipping craft.

"He's trying to head in toward the beach!" Pete said.

But the pilot could not make it. The helicopter dropped straight down into the big waves a hundred yards off shore!

CHAPTER 6

THE BASKET ELEVATOR

"WE MUST help those fliers!" Pam cried out, as the children gazed at the two men who had climbed to the top of the downed helicopter.

"Why don't they swim to shore?" said Ricky. "It's not far."

"They're probably hurt," Pete replied. "Come on, Carlos, let's swim out to them."

"Wait!" Pam said. "I see a boat." She pointed to a sandy knoll fifty feet away, where a rowboat lay overturned.

The children raced to the boat, which was large enough to hold five people. The three boys turned it over. Fortunately the oars were underneath.

"We'd better hurry!" Holly urged.

With all the children helping, the boat was dragged along the sandy beach and launched in the water.

61

"We'll save you in a minute!"

"You girls stay here," Pete said. "Ricky, Carlos, and I will row out."

"*Bueno*," said Maya. "I'll run and get Daddy."

As the girls shouted encouragement, the boys pushed the rowboat deeper into the surf, then jumped aboard.

Ricky sat in the stern while Pete and Carlos each manned an oar. With sure strokes they made their way toward the floating helicopter.

"Why hasn't it sunk?" Ricky asked Carlos as they drew closer to the craft.

"It's probably stuck on a sand bar."

"But the copter will be pounded to pieces by the waves if it's not pulled off soon," Pete said worriedly.

Now the boys could see why the men had not swum to shore. One of them had received a bad cut on his forehead, while the other was clutching an injured arm.

"We'll save you in a minute!" Pete called out as he and Carlos maneuvered the rowboat alongside the helicopter.

It was difficult bringing the small boat up to the aircraft. Finally Ricky reached out and grabbed hold of a corner of the cabin.

"That's swell, fellows," said one of the men as he and his companion slid off into the bottom of the rowboat.

While the boys rowed swiftly toward shore, the man, a slender, tan-skinned Puerto Rican, introduced himself as Señor Sifre. He said he thought his arm was broken.

"And I'm Ken Jones, an American pilot," said the other man. "Do you all live here?"

Pete quickly explained and added that Carlos' sister had gone for her father who was a doctor.

Señor Sifre said this was fine. Then he added that he operated pineapple plantations on Manati and on Vieques Island off the east coast.

"*Si,*" said Carlos. "My father has mentioned them."

"Ken was flying me from San Juan to Vieques," Señor Sifre explained, "when our engine failed."

"We were banged up when a big wave hit us," Jones said ruefully. "I'm still dizzy." He reached his hand over the side of the rowboat and dashed some salt water on his cut forehead.

When the rowboat touched the beach, Ricky hopped out and held it while Pete and Carlos assisted the rescued men to solid ground.

Dr. Villamil and Mr. Hollister had run to the beach with Maya and were awaiting the rescue boat. Quickly examining both men, the physician announced that Señor Sifre's arm had suffered a bad bruise but did not seem to broken. The pilot's head gash would require several stitches.

"Come to my home," he said, "and I will take care of the wound in my office."

"And will someone please notify the authorities of

the crash?" the pilot requested. "Ask to have a motor launch tow the copter ashore."

"I'll do that," Mr. Hollister offered.

As the children returned the rowboat to the spot where they had found it, the rescued men walked back to the doctor's office. They came out twenty minutes later. Señor Sifre's arm was in a sling and Ken Jones had a bandage on his forehead.

"I hope I may have an opportunity to do something for you children some day," Señor Sifre said, smiling. "Perhaps you will visit one of my pineapple plantations."

"We'd love to!" Pam exclaimed, and told of the wonderful pineapples they had received in Shoreham.

"Why, they came from my plantation at Manati," Señor Sifre said, laughing. "I remember the order."

Suddenly Carlos called out that the government launch was standing by the helicopter. The children and grownups all hurried back to the beach to watch the salvage operation. Lines were attached to the helicopter and in a few minutes the power boat had pulled it off the sand bar.

"The cabin is watertight, so she should make shore safely," the pilot said as the boat headed toward them. Finally the damaged helicopter was beached and pulled ashore just as mechanics arrived in a truck. They set to work immediately to repair the engine.

Holly and Ricky edged close to the workmen. One of them, a smiling young Puerto Rican named José, said, "How would you two like to be my helpers?"

"Yes!" exclaimed tomboy Holly eagerly.

"And me too!" Ricky chimed in.

"All right," the man said, pointing to his tool kit which lay nearby. "Please bring me a left-handed screw driver."

The brother and sister opened the lid of his green metal box and poked among the tools. There were two screw drivers.

"Which one is left-handed?" Holly whispered.

Ricky looked at both. They were identical. Then he said, "Holly, do you suppose the man's joking with us?"

"If he is," Holly replied, "I have an idea." Holding a screwdriver in each hand, she walked up to the workman.

"Did you find a left-handed one?" he asked.

Holly held out her hands. "The one in my left hand is left-handed," she said with a giggle, and everyone laughed.

"They outfoxed you that time, José," another workman jibed. "You're smart kids!"

A short while later, one of the workmen stepped inside the helicopter cabin and tested the rotor blades. They spun perfectly.

"We're all set to go again! Ready, Señor Sifre?" Ken called.

"*Si.*"

Señor Sifre thanked Dr. Villamil, Mr. Hollister, and the children for their help. "Don't forget you're

66

to visit me sometime," he said before he stepped into the cabin.

"We'll come!" they chorused.

As the children waved, the helicopter took off from the beach and headed over the ocean for Vieques Island.

"What a 'citing morning," Sue exclaimed as the mechanics drove off.

The children wanted to return to the mysterious stone, but just then Mrs. Villamil arrived to tell them luncheon was ready.

"We can examine the stone again after we eat," Carlos said. "Nobody will disturb it."

But after luncheon Mrs. Villamil told the others she had planned a tour of San Juan that afternoon for Mrs. Hollister and the children. Mr. Hollister would play golf with Dr. Villamil, who had the afternoon free.

The children glanced at one another. They would have to postpone their investigation until later.

"I think you'll love the old Spanish part of town with its narrow streets and little shops," Mrs. Villamil told them.

Soon the station wagon was traveling along a wide boulevard, past attractive white hotels on either side. Presently modern buildings gave way to old-fashioned structures of Spanish design. Mrs. Villamil parked the car in the center of old San Juan.

"Look at the pretty statue!" Holly cried out, pointing to a large bronze figure. The face of the statue looked familiar.

"I know who he is!" Ricky exclaimed. "Christopher Columbus!"

"This is called *Plaza Colon,* which means Columbus Plaza," Maya explained.

They walked about the square. The Hollister children were intrigued by the fact that the shops were entirely open in front. They had never seen this before. Presently Mrs. Villamil suggested that they walk to the historic old fort, El Morro.

"It's not far," she said, leading the Hollisters along a cobbled street. The sidewalks were so narrow that two people could hardly pass without bumping.

"This street was made for thin people," Holly remarked.

Small children played along both sides of the street. They spoke rapidly in Spanish as the Hollisters passed and stared at them shyly.

Mrs. Villamil turned a corner and started up a hilly street which was even narrower. At a house a few doors ahead stood a peddler beside a vegetable cart. He was calling to someone on the second-floor balcony.

Instantly the heads of two little girls about five years old appeared. They spoke in rapid Spanish to the man below.

"Their mother wants to buy some yucca," Carlos translated for the Hollisters.

"What's that?" Pete asked.

Maya explained that yucca is something like a sweet potato, but with a delicate flavor.

"Oh, look!" Sue cried as the native children began to lower a good-sized basket on the end of a long rope.

The peddler smiled as it reached him. He put his hand inside the basket and took out several coins. Then he placed several yucca in the container and the children hauled it back up to the balcony.

"What fun to do your shopping that way!" Pam said, chuckling, as the peddler trundled his cart along the street. "Let's try it in Shoreham."

"I wish they'd lower the basket again," said Holly.

Carlos called up something in Spanish. In a moment the basket was lowered once more while the two native children giggled. Inside it was a small doll dressed in a bright red skirt and blouse.

"They want you to see their toy," Maya explained.

"Oh, what lovely needlework!" Mrs. Hollister remarked, examining the doll's clothes after the children had passed the toy around. "I must buy Sue one like it."

Mrs. Villamil explained that San Juan girls sew very well and that doll making is one of their hobbies. Pam was the last to look at the toy. After admiring it she started to put it back in the basket.

"Wait a second," Pete requested.

He put a hand into his pocket and pulled out a nut candy bar he had bought at the New York airport. Placing this in the basket he motioned the children to haul it up.

When they saw their gift, the two little heads popped over the balcony, grinning. *"Gracias, Gracias!"*

"Is that 'thank you'?" Ricky asked Carlos.

"Sí. You're learning fast!"

"Bye now!" Holly waved, as the girls divided the candy.

The Hollisters and their friends walked on up the hill and turned to the left.

"The fortress is right ahead," Mrs. Villamil pointed out. "El Morro now is part of Fort Brooke, the U. S. Army post."

The Hollisters were passing an old whitewashed church when suddenly Mrs. Hollister turned around. "Where's Sue?" she asked.

Everyone looked. The little girl was not in sight.

"Oh dear," Mrs. Hollister said. "Where do you suppose Sue went?"

"I have an idea," Pam volunteered. She beckoned to the others. "Come, I'll show you."

Retracing her steps, Pam turned the corner and looked down the hillside street. Halfway along the block a crowd had gathered under the balcony where the two little girls had lowered the basket.

"If I know Sue——" said Pam.

Running down the street, she was first to reach the spot. Her sister was calling, *"Gracias, gracias,* pull real hard!"

The two little girls upstairs, assisted by an older brother, were pulling the basket up.

Inside of it sat Sue!

"Come down, please!" Mrs. Hollister called as she and the others pushed their way forward.

Suddenly the rope slipped from the children's hands. Sue and the basket plummeted toward the sidewalk!

CHAPTER 7

STONE HUNTERS

"OH!" SCREAMED Sue as the elevator basket hurtled toward the sidewalk. The children looked on in horror.

But Pete and Carlos sprang to action. Lunging forward, they caught the basket in outstretched arms. The impact rolled both boys to the ground and Sue tumbled on top of them.

Mrs. Hollister ran up. "Goodness, what a narrow escape!" she exclaimed. "Are you all right?"

The three children picked themselves up and nodded. Sue added, "I didn't get hurted 'cause Pete and Carlos were nice, soft pillows."

As the boys grinned and brushed themselves off, Mrs. Villamil praised them for their quick thinking. Carlos now called up to the balcony, advising the native children not to carry any more passengers in their elevator. They promised.

After zigzagging through several more narrow streets, the Villamils and Hollisters came to a large iron gate. A soldier was standing beside it.

"This is the entrance to Fort Brooke," Carlos said.

"The old Spanish fort, El Morro, is out there on that point of land."

Ricky saluted the sentry, who smartly returned it. "Have a good time exploring," the young soldier said, smiling.

Inside the gate and to the right, the Hollisters were amazed to see a broad sweeping plateau of green grass. It extended to a bluff overlooking the ocean.

"Why, it's a golf course!" Pam exclaimed.

Tiny flags fluttered from bamboo poles marking the various holes. Men and women in shorts and sport shirts were moving over the course.

Mrs. Villamil smiled and said, "Where there once were cannonballs, now there are golf balls!"

"I want to see some cannonballs," Ricky said as he ran ahead. The road was bordered on the left by U. S. Army buildings, and small homes for the officers and their families.

The children raced after Ricky and soon came to the tremendous old fortress—El Morro. Its massive stone walls rose high above the roaring surf.

"I see the cannons!" Holly cried. The big iron guns poked their black snouts through slits in the stone walls toward the water.

"Better not shoot them off, Ricky," Carlos said with a wink at Pete. "You might hit a whale."

Ricky grinned, but Sue took Carlos seriously. "Please don't hurt the poor whale," she begged.

Pete admired the ancient masonry. How thick the walls were! "Those old Spaniards sure knew

74

"I wonder how far down it is."

how to build. No cannonball could get through here."

"And nobody could climb up from the sea, either," Maya said. She pointed to the parapet, which dropped off abruptly to the waterfront far below.

"Hmm, I wonder how far down it is," Ricky said. Before anyone could stop him, he ran toward the outer wall.

"Stop!" Mrs. Hollister commanded.

Ricky had no intention of dropping off into the sea, but he gave the others a good fright. He stopped inches from the precipice and peered down. Far below, the water foamed over the coral rocks.

"Don't frighten us again like that," Mrs. Hollister said sternly, and Ricky promised.

"If you want to get a different view of the fort," Mrs. Villamil suggested, "go to that old sentry tower over there."

She pointed to a small circular structure with a round stone roof protruding from one corner of the fort and overlooking the ocean.

Pete and Pam were the first to reach it. Suddenly they realized that two men were inside talking in loud voices. They did not notice the Hollisters, who could not help overhearing the men's conversation.

"We can't search here!" one of them said angrily. "The soldiers won't let us."

"I do not think the stone is in the fort anyway," the other fellow said. He spoke with a Spanish accent.

"But we've looked all the way from here to Lizard Cove! It has to be somewhere."

At the mention of Lizard Cove, Pete turned and signaled the other children to approach quietly. They crept up.

Pam whispered to her brother, "What stone do you suppose they mean?"

"Sh!" Pete nudged her, as the voices continued.

"I am tired of looking for the treasure," said the Puerto Rican.

"We'd better not give up now."

"But we have no money."

"We'll manage. Let's return to Lizard Cove and start to search again."

"Okay," the native said in a grumbling tone and stepped from the sentry box.

He was a short man, slightly bald, with black hair. He glared at the children with black, shifty eyes. "Hey, Stilts, these kids have been spying on us!" he told his friend.

The second man stepped out. He was tall and thin, with very long legs. His shoulders looked bony through an open-collared shirt and his small head gave him an owlish appearance.

"I told you to be on the lookout!" he chided his companion. Then he turned to Pete. "Did you hear what we were saying?"

"Only a few words," the boy replied honestly.

Both men looked relieved and the smaller fellow said something in Spanish.

"Okay, Umberto," the tall one replied.

As they hurried off over the cobbled courtyard of the fort, Pete noticed that the shorter man limped slightly. When they were out of earshot, he quickly related the mysterious conversation the other children had not heard.

"Could it be our stone they're looking for?" Carlos wondered. "It's an odd one——"

"It *could* be," Pete said. "Let's hurry back and hide the stone. It must be important."

Mrs. Hollister and Mrs. Villamil, who had been strolling leisurely, now came up to where the children were discussing the rude strangers. They were amazed to hear what had happened.

"Pete's right," Mrs. Hollister said. "We'd better go back."

On the return route through Fort Brooke, the children kept a sharp watch for the two men, but they were nowhere in sight.

"I hope we never see them again," Pam said with a shudder. "They gave me the creeps."

After passing a lovely tropical garden, the children left Fort Brooke by a different exit. As they went through the gate, Pete noticed two boys about twelve years old seated on the curb near the gate. One of them was weeping.

"I think they're blind," Maya whispered softly.

"Are they Puerto Ricans?" Pete asked.

Carlos nodded. Then he addressed the blind boys in Spanish. After an exchange of conversation, Carlos

78

told the others that the boys' names were Manuel and Desi. They were from the school for the blind at Santurce.

"Manuel's guitar has just been stolen," Carlos informed them. "That is why he is crying." Carlos went on to translate what Manuel had said. The instrument was a very special one inherited by the boy from his grandfather.

"How sad to lose such a prized possession!" Mrs. Hollister said sympathetically.

"We'll try to find it for you," Holly told the blind boy as he turned his head toward them and managed a smile.

"Thank you. See, I can speak English too!" he said.

"How long ago was your guitar stolen?" Pete asked, wondering where to look first.

Manuel said that it had been taken about five minutes before. He had laid it down on the grass while he went to a nearby drinking fountain. When he returned, it was gone.

"I heard two men walk by me," Desi said in English, "while I waited for Manuel here. One of them might have taken the guitar."

"If so, then the thief can't be far from here," Pam said. "It might have been one of the two men we saw who called themselves Stilts and Umberto. They said they needed money. Perhaps they stole the guitar to sell it!"

"May we run ahead and look for them, Mother?" Pete begged.

"Yes, but be careful."

"We'll come with you," Carlos and Maya said, as the Hollister children started off.

Sue remained with her mother. The six other children hurried off in the direction of the old city.

"This is exciting," said Maya as they ran along. "We've never played detective before."

"Tell us what to do," Carlos requested.

Pete said they should question passers-by first. They did this, the Hollisters in English and their friends in Spanish. Nobody had seen a man with a guitar. Finally Carlos asked a barefoot young boy playing near the curb.

The little fellow replied excitedly in Spanish and Carlos translated. "Yes, he just saw a man with a guitar. He and a companion went down this side street."

Running pell-mell, the six children rounded the corner. "I see him," Pam called out a few seconds later.

Far ahead, rapidly cutting in and out among the pedestrians, was a tall man. He carried a guitar in one hand.

"Is that Stilts?" Pete asked, putting on more speed.

"I can't tell," Pam replied breathlessly.

Hearing the excited shouts of the children, the fugitive ran faster. But he did not look back.

"Stop him! Stop that thief!" Carlos shouted, as they gained on the fellow.

A man reached for the fleeing figure, but the thief dodged in time to avoid him. The fellow disappeared around the next corner. As the children turned into the street, a fruit vendor pushed his cart into the narrow roadway, blocking traffic.

"Watch out, Pete!" yelled Holly. Her brother was in the lead.

Pete was running so fast, however, that he could not stop in time. He bumped squarely into the cart, tilting it wildly!

CHAPTER 8

PLAYING DETECTIVE

CRASH! The vendor's cart tumbled on its side, spilling all the fruits and vegetables into the cobbled street.

As oranges, grapefruit, bananas, and pineapples rolled along the curb, the peddler waved his arms and shouted in a high-pitched voice. The Hollisters could not understand a word but knew he was very angry.

Holly grasped Maya's hand. "Will he hurt us?" she asked in a frightened voice.

"Don't worry," Maya whispered. "He's only saying we should watch where we're going."

"Tell him I'm sorry," Pete said. "I didn't mean to do it."

Carlos made the apology, then he and Pete quickly righted the cart. All the children busily gathered up the fallen fruit.

Ricky, in his zeal to help, suddenly turned too quickly. He stepped on a bunch of ripe, red bananas and sat down hard, the bananas under him! Squash! They were ruined!

The vendor wrung his hands and cried out again,

Crash! The vendor's cart tumbled on its side.

his voice rising even higher. Seeing what had happened, Pam took some coins from her pocket and offered to pay for the ruined fruit.

This made the peddler feel better. *"Gracias, gracias,"* he said bowing and, taking the money, he smiled for the first time.

When everything had been picked up, Carlos told the man the children had been chasing a thief.

The vendor's eyes widened. "A thief, you say? Was that the fellow running with the guitar?"

"He's the one," Carlos said.

"Where did he go?" Maya asked.

The peddler pointed excitedly to a shop a few yards along *Calle San Justo.* He said a tall fellow had ducked into the open doorway leading to the second floor.

"Maybe we can still catch him!" Pete cried out after Carlos translated the conversation. "Let's go!"

They hurried past the shop and stepped inside the cool, dark hallway. No one was there.

"Maybe the thief lives upstairs," Pam suggested.

Quietly the children climbed the steps. The door of the second-floor apartment stood wide open. Carlos called out a greeting. There was no answer from inside.

"We dare not go in," Maya warned.

Pete walked farther along the dim hallway. "Say, look!" he said in an excited whisper. "There's a rear stairway. Maybe the thief went down there. Come on!"

The children hurried down the steps, which led into a narrow alley. A small boy and girl were playing in it with their dog.

"Did you see a tall man with a guitar come out here?" Carlos asked them in Spanish.

The children said no.

"Let's go back," Pete suggested, disappointed.

They mounted the steps to the upstairs hallway, then started to descend to the street.

"What shall we do now?" Pam asked.

Pete thought they had better tell the police about the stolen guitar, then go home. "If Stilts and Umberto are looking for a treasure stone, we'd better hurry and protect ours."

Just then Holly glanced up the stairs. "Look, she shouted, "a man is going down the hall!"

Pete bounded up the flight two steps at a time. Reaching the top, he heard footsteps on the back stairway.

"Somebody must have been hiding in the apartment," he thought.

By the time the boy reached the back alley and looked about, no one was in sight except the two children and their dog. Seconds later Carlos was at Pete's side. He asked the children once more if they had seen a man run by with a guitar.

"Yes, and he was in a big hurry," the little boy said. "He disappeared in the direction of *Calle Luna*."

Pete and Carlos dashed after him, but *Calle Luna*

was so crowded with pedestrians and sightseers that speed afoot was impossible. The fellow's getaway had been complete.

Pete was glum as he and Carlos joined the others. They retraced their steps to the place where their mothers were anxiously waiting with Manuel and Desi.

The women were amazed to hear what had happened and agreed that the police should be notified. Carlos spotted a tall young policeman strolling along *Calle Christo.*

"*Mira! Mira!*" he called out.

"That means 'look here,' " Maya said as the officer hurried over to them.

After introductions, Carlos explained about Manuel's stolen guitar. The officer, Tomas Gonzalez, made notes and said he would report the theft immediately. The children thanked him and he hurried off.

Taking the two blind boys by the hand, Pam and Maya led them to the Villamil car. Soon they were riding along the streets of Santurce toward the school for the blind.

Ricky happened to glance out the rear window and noticed a cab behind them. Whenever Mrs. Villamil turned, so did the taxi.

"Say, Pete," Ricky whispered, "I think we're being followed."

When Pete looked out the window, the cab dropped back behind a truck and was not seen again.

"I guess the driver knows we caught on," he said.

Fifteen minutes later Mrs. Villamil stopped the car in front of a quadrangle of white frame cottages.

"This is the school for the blind," she said.

Through the gateway to the grounds the Hollisters saw tall palm trees and shrubs with bright orange-colored blossoms.

"What a lovely place!" Mrs. Hollister remarked.

Here and there on benches alongside the walks sat groups of blind boys and girls playing guitars and singing lovely songs in harmony.

"These are my friends," Manuel told the Villamils in Spanish and Carlos translated. "We always sing together. It's fun."

Now that Manuel and Desi were on home ground, they knew every inch of the way. Without hesitation they led their new-found friends to a long, low building at the far end of the quadrangle.

Entering the building, the blind boys took the Hollisters and the Villamils into the office. There they introduced everyone to a small, kindly-looking dark-haired woman named Mrs. Sandoz, who was the school's director.

The woman was shocked to hear of the theft of Manuel's guitar. "It was very valuable," she said. "I do hope the police will catch the thief."

"But if they don't," Ricky spoke up, "maybe we can buy Manuel a new guitar."

"You are kind children," Mrs. Sandoz said. "Come, let me show you around our school."

As they walked down a corridor, the woman told them there were about ninety pupils who came from all over the island of Puerto Rico.

"Here are some of our children," Mrs. Sandoz said as she opened a door to a small classroom. Inside a group of six-year-olds sat around a small table with a young, attractive woman.

The Hollisters could see that the teacher also was blind. On hearing them enter, the young woman arose. Introduced, she explained that these children came from the interior of Puerto Rico and were learning to speak English.

"What have you learned today?" the teacher asked a little dark-skinned girl named Anna.

Anna stood up and in a clear voice said, "I-have-a-cat."

"Oh, so do we!" Holly spoke up. "Her name is White Nose and she's black!"

"She has five kittens," Sue added.

The teacher asked the Hollisters to repeat very slowly what they had just said. Holly and Sue did so and the little blind children chuckled.

"They understand us!" Holly said happily.

Then Anna, who spoke English better than the others, reached into her desk and pulled out a little lizard. "See my pet," she said.

"Oh," Holly cried. "He's just like Lucky!"

When Sue saw Anna's pet her eyes filled with tears. "I want Lucky back!" she quavered, biting her lips.

As Pam comforted her sister, it suddenly grew dark outside.

"Here comes one of our famous Puerto Rican showers," Maya said.

"And I left our car windows open!" Mrs. Villamil exclaimed.

"I'll close them, Mother," Carlos said.

"Let me help you!" Pam volunteered.

"Okay, come on!"

The boy and girl ran across the quadrangle just as a few big drops splattered to the sidewalk.

They were nearly to the car when Pam grabbed Carlos' arm. "Look!" she exclaimed.

The hood of their car was up and a short man standing in the road was looking into the engine.

"Hey!" Carlos called in Spanish. "What are you doing?"

The fellow alongside the car did not turn his head but ran off just as the rain pelted down.

"I wonder who he was," Pam said as they reached the station wagon. "He looked like Umberto."

By now the children were drenched. Pam started to roll up the windows while Carlos closed the hood. Then he got inside to help Pam.

"What did he do to the motor?" Pam asked.

Carlos said he did not see that any damage had been done. "We'll have to wait until the rain is over and have Mother try it," he said.

In a few minutes the downpour ended as suddenly

as it had started. The clouds rolled away and the sun shone brilliantly again.

Carlos and Pam stepped out of the car, their clothes still damp.

"Here come the others," Pam said as she looked across the quadrangle.

When Pam explained what had happened, Mrs. Villamil got into the driver's seat, inserted the key, and tried to start the engine. There was no response.

"That man tried to sabotage us," Pete said. "Let me look at the motor."

Pete liked to tinker with cars and often helped his father work on their station wagon. He got out and lifted the hood. After looking over the engine for a few minutes he exclaimed, "I've found the trouble."

"What is it?" Carlos asked.

"A wire to the battery was disconnected," Pete replied. He replaced it and the motor started instantly.

"Why did that man want to play a mean trick like that on us?" Mrs. Villamil asked as they started off.

"To delay us," Pete replied worriedly. "Mrs. Villamil, I'm afraid he was Umberto. Will you please go to Lizard Cove as fast as possible?"

Mrs. Villamil did as the boy requested, taking the shortest route to her home. It had grown so warm after the sudden rain that Carlos' and Pam's clothes were nearly dry by the time Mrs. Villamil pulled into their driveway.

"Come on, Carlos," Pete said as they got out of the car. "Let's examine our stone right away!"

All the children except Sue ran to the spot where they had left the stone. It was not there!

"Someone has stolen it!" Pam wailed.

CHAPTER 9

A SLIPPERY BANISTER

THE mystery stone gone!

"We shouldn't have left it unguarded!" Pete moaned as he gazed at the hole in the sand.

Pam quickly glanced around, noting several sets of footprints. And about ten feet away she saw something which made her cry out.

"Look at these tracks!"

As the others crowded around they could plainly see a wide trail through the sand. Apparently it had been made by one end of a board being dragged along the beach.

Pete snapped his fingers. "I have it!" he said. "Two people picked up the stone to carry it off but it was too heavy. So they put it on the end of a board and pulled it away."

"Stilts and Umberto!" Carlos guessed.

The others agreed and Pam said, "We shouldn't have any trouble finding them. The board marks lead up the beach."

After following the tracks for a quarter of a mile, the children came upon four boys. All of them between ten and twelve years of age, were busy making a fort of stones and driftwood.

"Maybe they know something about our mystery stone," Holly said in a low voice as they approached.

"Hello there!" Pete called out.

"Hi!" replied the tallest one, a boy with straight blond hair. He was laying a water-soaked plank on top of several pieces of wood.

"That's a fine fort you're building," Pete said in a friendly voice.

"You like it, eh?" the blond boy answered in English. "We've been working on it all day. We want to play battle before we fly back to New York tomorrow."

"We just came from there," Pam spoke up.

"Where do you live?" Ricky asked them.

"Boston," one of the other boys said. "Bob and I are cousins."

Bob asked, "Would you like to help us with our fort?"

Pete thanked him but explained that they were looking for a large stone that had been taken from Dr. Villamil's beach.

"Golly, was that your stone?" Bob said, looking a little frightened.

"Yes, it was," Carlos spoke up. "If you took it by mistake, that's all right. But we would like to have it back."

Bob explained that they had been looking for material with which to build their fort. "It was a swell stone," he said, "but too heavy for us to carry. We had to drag it across the beach on a board."

Bob walked around to the front of the fort, pointed. "We used it right here as the cornerstone."

The Hollisters and their friends thought they would have the stone back in a minute, but puzzled expressions came over their faces. They could not see the mystery stone.

"It's not here," Carlos said with a questioning look.

Bob looked sheepish. "I'm sorry," he said, "but we don't have the stone any more."

"What happened to it?" Ricky asked.

"We sold it."

"What!" Pete exclaimed.

Bob said that while the boys were building their fort two men had walked along the beach apparently looking for something. When she heard this, Pam's face flushed.

"Was one tall and the other short?" she asked excitedly.

"Yes," Bob replied. "Do you know them?"

"I think we do," Pete said. "Tell us what happened then."

Bob said that the men had wandered over to see the fort and had suddenly spied the cornerstone.

"Before we could do anything about it," Bob said, "they dragged the stone out and looked it over."

"Yes?" Holly prodded as Bob paused.

"The men said they wanted to buy the stone,"

Bob said. "I thought if it were so valuable maybe we should keep it. But the smaller man said something in Spanish and shook his fist at us. Then the tall man gave us fifty cents and between the two of them they carried the stone away."

"Where did they take it?" Pam asked.

The boys pointed far up the beach. "The last I saw of them they were in front of that hotel. Perhaps they're staying there."

Bob offered to give Carlos the fifty cents he had received for the stone. But the Puerto Rican boy would not accept it.

"Anyway, your information has been worth plenty to us," he said. "Come on," he called to Maya and the Hollisters, "let's hurry to the hotel."

Saying good-by to the boys from Boston, they hurried across the sand toward the hotel. It was a long, white, five-story building which faced the ocean. At one end of it the children could see people lounging about a swimming pool.

"What will we do if we find Stilts and Umberto?" Maya asked. She was becoming a little frightened over the detective work.

"Don't worry," Pete said. "There are six of us and lots of people at the hotel."

Though the Hollisters were intent upon their job, they did notice the attractive lawn in front of the hotel. The trade winds blowing in from the Atlantic Ocean were bending the palm trees and the beautiful flowering bushes.

With Pete and Carlos in the lead, the young sleuths hurried into the busy lobby of the hotel. Guests were coming and going and smartly dressed bellhops were carrying luggage in and out of the building. In the center of the lobby was a large, glass-topped table surrounded by half a dozen wrought-iron chairs. Men and women sat there chatting, but although the children searched every face, not one of the guests in any way resembled Stilts or Umberto.

"Maybe those men didn't come into the hotel after all," Ricky said.

"Or else they went to their room," Pam suggested. "Let's ask the clerk if they're registered here."

"They wouldn't give a name like Stilts," Ricky said.

"No, but Umberto might be the other man's right name," his sister replied.

After waiting for several guests to register, Pete approached the clerk, a handsome young man in a dark jacket. A small sign on the counter said his name was Señor Felippe.

"Is anybody staying here by the name of Umberto?" Pete asked him.

"Is that his first or last name?" the clerk said, looking down at his register.

"We don't know," Pete answered. He gave a brief description of Umberto and also Stilts.

"I'm sorry," Señor Felippe said. "I don't recall anyone fitting those descriptions registering here."

"We thought they came into this hotel a few minutes ago," Maya spoke up.

"Perhaps they did," the clerk said. "Have you looked around the mezzanine floor?" He pointed to a marble circular stairway leading to the second floor. "Maybe your friends are relaxing up there," he said, smiling.

"Friends!" Holly said hotly.

Señor Felippe looked questioningly at the children, who thanked him and hurried to the mezzanine stairs. A smooth iron railing spiraled upward on either side of the marble steps.

As they started up, Holly and Ricky dropped behind the others. The same thought was running through their minds.

"Wouldn't this be a dandy slide?" tomboy Holly said, bursting into a grin.

"Swell!" Ricky agreed.

By now the two children were at the top of the stairway. They glanced down. Nothing was below them except a row of palms potted in wooden tubs, which decorated the base of the stairway.

"Now?" Holly asked.

"Go ahead," Ricky said.

The girl flung a leg over the banister. Then, lying against it, she started to slide slowly.

"Go on, faster!" Ricky said.

Holly, who was holding on with her hands and knees, loosened her grip a little and zipped down the banister. Nearing the bottom, she gathered too much

She landed kerplunk.

speed and—whiz—slipped off. She landed *kerplunk* on a potted palm, which toppled over.

For a moment Holly sat on the floor, dazed, her legs stretched in front of her and her arms flung out behind. Ricky raced down the steps to help his sister. He arrived at her side just as the clerk came upon the scene.

"What's going on here?" the young man asked.

As he helped Holly to her feet, she said, "I—I was sliding too fast."

"Yes, you were. Are you hurt?"

Holly felt herself in several places, then shook her head and smiled. "I'm all right, thank you."

Señor Felippe chuckled and said to Ricky, "I think you have in mind doing the same thing. But please do not."

Ricky promised not to slide down the banister and assisted the clerk in setting the palm back where it belonged. Then he and Holly went upstairs to find the other children. No guests were there.

"We were looking for you," Pam said as they met her. "Where have you been?"

"Playing," Ricky said. "Did you see the men who took the stone?"

"We've looked all around here and can't find them," Pam answered.

Just then Carlos emerged from a narrow hallway at the west end of the mezzanine.

"Pst!" he said, and beckoned to the others.

The children excitedly followed him. "Did you find them?" Pete whispered.

"Yes!" Carlos said excitedly. "Alongside a telephone booth."

"You're getting to be a fine detective," Pam told the boy as they tiptoed down the hall to the booth, which stood against one wall about halfway down the hallway. The men were out of sight on the far side of it.

The children burst upon the two men who were kneeling to examine the mystery stone. Stilts and Umberto were so startled that they leaped up, their mouths opening in amazement.

"Where did you come from?" Stilts said, scowling.

"We want our stone," Pete told him. "It was taken from the Villamils' property at Lizard Cove."

"Your stone!" Umberto said indignantly. "We bought this."

"We know that," Pete said as he put his hand into his pocket. "Anyhow, here's the fifty cents you paid for it. Now give the stone to us."

"Try and get it," Stilts said, leering down at them.

"You'll give it back and the guitar too!" Pam cried out.

The tall man's eyes widened, giving his face a buglike look. Umberto started to say something in Spanish, but Stilts whirled on him.

"Keep still!" he ordered. Then he turned to the children. "What do you mean—guitar?"

"You took it from the blind boy," Holly said.

"Come on, let's get out of here," Stilts said, nudging his friend.

As he bent over to pick up the mystery stone, Carlos put one foot on it. "No you don't—it belongs to us."

With the six children pressing in on them, the two men realized they would not have an easy time making off with the heavy stone.

"What's on it that's so valuable?" Pete asked as Stilts bent down to glance at the rock again.

"That's our business," he replied. "Now come on and get out of here before I call the manager." When the children refused to move, he turned to Umberto. "Guard the stone. I'll be back soon."

Stilts pushed his way through the knot of children and hurried up the hall. Looking over his shoulder, he cried out, "I'll fix you!"

CHAPTER 10

THE SECRET

FOR a couple of seconds the Hollister and Villamil children stood stunned by the turn of events. Then their courage returned.

"Girls, follow Stilts and see what he's going to do," Pete suggested. "We boys will keep Umberto from moving this stone."

Pam hurried off with Holly and Maya. At the top of the stairs they saw Stilts go from the steps directly to the desk and speak to Señor Felippe. The clerk nodded and went into an office. In a moment he appeared with a gray-haired man and all three of them came toward the stairway.

"Stilts is going to have those men make us leave," Maya said worriedly.

Holly set her jaw determinedly. "*Nobody* can chase us out until we get the stone!" she said.

"That's right," Pam agreed. "When the hotel men hear our story they'll let us take the stone."

Pam's heart pounded as she hurried back to the boys, followed by Holly and Maya. In a few moments the three men arrived.

"There they are!" Stilts said as he pointed to the Hollisters and their friends.

The desk clerk raised his eyebrows when he saw Ricky and Holly. "Getting into more trouble?" he asked, looking surprised.

"We didn't do anything—honest!" Holly said, as the children turned to face the hotel men.

The gray-haired man spoke up. "I'm Señor Gregora, the manager of this hotel," he said. "What seems to be the trouble?"

Stilts spoke up quickly, saying that he and Umberto had bought the stone on the beach and that now these children were claiming it and not allowing the men to take the stone away.

Umberto said something in Spanish which made Carlos' eyes blaze. "We are not thieves!" he cried out. "You are the thieves!"

Señor Gregora laid a hand on the boy's shoulder. "We'll hear your side too," he said.

With a nod from Maya and Carlos, Pete acted as spokesman for the group and told the whole story. He also mentioned their suspicion that Stilts had stolen the blind boy's guitar.

"Nonsense!" snapped Stilts. "We know nothing about a guitar——"

"It's very dangerous to accuse people of theft," the manager said, "unless you have proof."

"This stone belongs to Carlos and Maya. I know that," Pete said. "But I can't prove the part about the guitar."

Señor Gregora turned to Stilts. "What room are you staying in here?" he asked unexpectedly.

Stilts and Umberto exchanged quick, sly glances. "We're in 810," Stilts replied.

The gray-haired man raised his eyebrows. "Really? That's strange. There isn't any eighth floor."

Stilts' chalky face flushed and the desk clerk added, "I've never seen these men before, Señor Gregora. I'm certain they're not registered here."

"This becomes more interesting," the manager said, looking at Stilts and Umberto suspiciously.

Maya looked up into Señor Gregora's face and said in a pleading voice, "We are telling the truth. The stone came from our property."

"And what is your name, may I ask?" the manager said.

"Maya Villamil."

"Any relation to the doctor?"

"He's our father," Carlos spoke up.

Stilts and Umberto stirred uneasily, watching the expression on the hotel manager's face.

"Dr. Villamil! Why, I am one of his patients," Señor Gregora said.

Stilts stooped to lift the stone. "Let's get out of here, Umberto," he said. "He's fallen for the kids' story."

"Not so fast," the manager told him. "We can

105

settle this by having Dr. Villamil come over here himself."

Now Stilts and Umberto looked worried. "Okay, Umberto," Stilts said, straightening his skinny frame. "Let's get out of this cheap hotel!"

"And I recommend that you don't come back," the manager said sternly.

Stilts and Umberto turned their backs and hurried down the hallway. The Puerto Rican, limping a little, had trouble keeping up with the taller man.

Carlos dashed after them to see where they were going and stood nearby as they hailed a taxi. In a few minutes the boy went back to the other children who were trying to figure out how to move the stone.

"I am becoming a detective," he said. "I overheard Umberto say something very important."

"What was it?" Pam asked.

"He said, 'We do not need the stone any more. We have the information we want.' "

"What did he mean by that?" Ricky asked.

"I don't know," Carlos said, unless Umberto figured out the inscription." He bent down to help Pete lift the heavy stone.

"We had better go home in a cab," Maya suggested.

"Yes," Señor Gregora said. The clerk had already gone back to the desk.

The children thanked the manager, who in turn lent a hand to the boys in carrying the stone to the street.

"I hope everything will be all right," the man said, as Carlos went for a taxi.

When the cab drove up Pete, Carlos, and Ricky put the stone on the floor of the back seat. The two older boys sat with the driver, while Ricky and the three girls squeezed into the rear seat.

When they arrived at the Villamil home, Carlos paid the driver, then the boys lifted the mystery stone to the ground. As the taxi drove away, Sue dashed out of the house and ran toward them. She asked where the others had been and they told her.

"Come see my surprise!" she cried out when they finished.

"Where is it?" Holly asked her sister.

"In the house. Come with me!"

"Did Mother buy you a Spanish doll?" Pam suggested.

"No. It's not like that," Sue replied as she tugged at her two sisters' hands.

She led them into the living room, with Maya following. She pointed to a low bowl on a table. Inside the bowl were some sand and a few leaves. And standing on one of the leaves was a lizard with a blue bow on his tail.

"Lucky!" Holly shrieked happily. "Lucky's back!"

"Oh, I'm so glad!" Pam said. "Where did you find him?"

Sue answered proudly. "In the fruit dish on the coffee table over there," she replied, skipping over to an attractive low bamboo table.

"Lucky's back!"

In the center of it was a brightly colored pottery bowl filled with tropical fruit. Sue pointed to the crown of a pineapple which rose high in the center of the bowl.

"This is where I found Lucky," she said gleefully.

By this time the boys had lugged the stone into the entrance hall. They now came to see what Sue's surprise was.

"Lucky!" exclaimed Ricky. "I thought he had run away!"

Sue proudly told him that Lucky liked the Hollisters better than the iguana lizards. "So he 'cided to live with us—see?"

Pete had a suggestion. "We'll let Lucky loose every morning to find his breakfast," he said. "After he eats, he'll come back home."

"No," Sue said determinedly. "I'll find the bugs and the worms for him to eat. Lucky will never leave us again."

With that she went over and picked the pet out of the bowl, putting him into her dress pocket. Lucky poked his head out and looked about.

"He likes it," Sue said, giggling.

At this moment Mr. and Mrs. Hollister and Dr. and Mrs. Villamil entered the room, and a maid came to say that the evening dinner was served. During the meal the children related the story of the stone and what had happened at the hotel.

"How exciting!" said Mrs. Villamil. "It was quite an adventure for my children."

Dr. Villamil became very much interested. "I have a suggestion to make," he said. "Since it is so hard to read the inscription on the stone, suppose I make a plaster mold of it. Whatever is on the face of the stone will show up much better that way."

"Oh, Daddy, that will be wonderful!" Maya exclaimed. Then her face clouded. "But Umberto said he knew what was on it. Maybe we should look again."

"I doubt that those men really read the inscription," her father said.

"*Bueno, bueno!*" Holly chirped, and her family smiled at her use of the Spanish word.

The physician went on to say that he had some plaster in his workshop in the basement.

"I can use that," he said, "and make an impression in a short time."

The children were so excited they could hardly wait to finish their supper. When it was over the doctor disappeared into his workshop and returned presently with some wet plaster.

The boys carried the stone out to the patio where the physician spread the soft white material onto the carved face of the rock.

"It will have to set for a while," Dr. Villamil said.

Mr. Hollister smiled and said that doctors are very often helpful in solving mysteries.

Carlos laughed. "All the Villamils will be detectives in a few days."

After the plaster had set Dr. Villamil removed it

from the stone. The indentations in the mystery rock had made high spots in the plaster.

"Now," he said, "if you will rub a crayon on these high portions and then hold the plaster cast up to a mirror, you should have the answer to your puzzle."

Maya hurried into the children's playroom and returned with a handful of crayons. Quickly she covered the raised portion of the plaster cast, then her father carried the cast inside to a mirror over the dining room buffet. The others had followed and now everyone studied the strange inscription.

"Look!" Pete said. "It's a rough outline of Puerto Rico!"

Beneath the crude map was an inscription in Spanish. Carlos whistled.

"It says, '*La corona de esmeraldas de la Infanta.*' That means the Infanta's emerald crown!"

"What's an *infanta?*" Holly asked.

Maya quickly explained that *infanta* was a Spanish word for royal princess.

Under the words was an arrow pointing to the south coast of Puerto Rico. Dr. Villamil spoke up. "It seems to indicate the town of Ponce," he said.

"Then the princess' crown is hidden somewhere in Ponce?" Pam said.

"It could be," Dr. Villamil said, and was about to go on, when they all heard a noise at the open window behind them.

Sue was the first to whirl about. "I—I saw somebody's head!" she cried out. "He was looking in!"

111

Everyone was alarmed. Had the eavesdropper learned their secret!

CHAPTER 11

A POLICEMAN CALLS

THE Hollisters and the Villamils rushed outside the house to look for the eavesdropper. Pete and Carlos heard a slight rustling noise in the bushes near the window. They dashed over to investigate, but whoever had been there had scurried away into the darkness.

"Have you a flashlight, Carlos?" Pete asked. "We'll trail him!"

"Yes. In my room." He dashed off to get it, returning in a few seconds. "Here it is, Pete."

As the grownups and the other children watched intently, Pete swung the light over the ground beneath the window. In the soft earth prints of the intruder's shoes were plainly visible.

"Look at these two that are right together," Pam said, bending down to examine them more closely. "They're left and right shoes and one print is deeper than the other."

"Perhaps they were made by a man with a limp," Dr. Villamil suggested.

"Umberto!" Pete exclaimed. "Crickets, if he has

113

discovered our secret he may find the emerald crown before we do."

"We won't let him!" Holly declared. "Please, Dad, can't we go right away and look for it?"

Mr. Hollister laid a hand on his small daughter's shoulder. "Not until tomorrow. But I'm sure Umberto can't start a search before morning, either."

Pete and Carlos followed the footprints to the road. Here they were lost and there was no sign of the eavesdropper. When everyone went indoors again, Dr. Villamil said, "We must notify the police at once about the eavesdropper."

"I'll do it, Dad," Carlos volunteered, and hurried off to the telephone. When he returned to the others he said, "A detective is coming to guard our home for the rest of the night."

"That is good," said Dr. Villamil. "When I was interrupted by that eavesdropper, I was about to tell you the old legend of the emerald treasure. Would you like to hear it?"

"Oh yes," all the children chorused.

Dr. Villamil stated that several hundred years before, a princess had been kidnaped and whisked away from Madrid by a band of fierce pirates. A ransom note was left by them demanding her priceless emerald crown as payment for her return.

"Was the poor princess ever found?" Holly asked.

Dr. Villamil explained that according to the legend she had been safely returned and the villains had received the emerald crown, according to the bargain.

"But the treasure did them no good," he went on. "The pirates fought and killed one another until only one burly brigand was left. He became known as the Green Pirate because he possessed the green gems."

The doctor added that once the Green Pirate nearly lost the treasure while engaging in some pirating along the coast. "He was in a fierce sea battle and was lucky to remain alive. All that happened to him was that he lost his right leg. But the story goes that he soon acquired a peg leg and hid the small emerald crown in the upper part of it."

"Oh boy!" Ricky said. "All we have to do is find the peg leg and we'll have the treasure."

"Let's go to Ponce!" Pete said eagerly.

"Tomorrow morning!" Holly urged.

The children rose early next day and had breakfast. They were all eager to be on their way to Ponce to search for the treasure before Stilts and Umberto had a chance to find it.

Suddenly the telephone rang. Carlos answered. Holding his hand over the mouthpiece, he whispered to the others:

"It's the police."

After he had spoken in Spanish for a while he hung up excitedly. "They've found two men they think are Stilts and Umberto!" he said.

"Yikes!" Ricky exclaimed gleefully. "Now we can look for the treasure all by ourselves."

"And make those bad men give back the stolen guitar," Holly added.

Carlos smiled. "First we have to identify them," he said. "The police want us to come over to headquarters right away."

The older children piled into the station wagon and Mr. Hollister drove them to headquarters. They all hurried inside and were met at the desk by a sergeant named Rine.

"I think I have the men you children are looking for," he said, "although they deny that they are guilty."

"Where did you arrest them?" Pete asked.

"At a bus stop near Lizard Cove late last night."

"Where are they now?" Pam asked.

The sergeant nodded toward a door at the left side of his desk. "Come this way," he said. "They're waiting inside."

He arose and ushered the children into a small room. In the center of it sat two men at a table. Pam was crestfallen when she saw them.

"They're not the right ones!"

"No, they aren't," Pete agreed. "There's been some mistake. But they do look something like Stilts and Umberto."

"I told you we're innocent," the taller prisoner said. "Just because I'm from the States and my friend's a Puerto Rican and we were in trouble once before——"

"All right," the sergeant said. "We're sorry we picked you up. But we couldn't take any chances."

The Hollisters, too, offered their apologies to the

two men. Pam told them the story of the stolen guitar and they seemed sympathetic.

The taller man said, "Say, we did see two other guys who looked something like us."

"When? Where?" Pete asked.

The man said they had noticed the fellows at an all-night diner and told the location.

"Let's go there and investigate," Carlos said, feeling like a real detective.

After the prisoners were released, the children thanked the police sergeant, then drove to the diner. Pete and Carlos went in. The night counterman, named Raul, stout and bald-headed, was just about to leave. When Pete questioned him, he admitted serving two men answering the description of Stilts and Umberto.

"Did you overhear anything they said?" Pete asked.

Raul pulled on his lower lip as he searched his memory. "Yes, they did say something unusual."

"What was it?" Pam asked, her heart pounding.

"I didn't hear all of it," Raul replied, "but the tall one said something about a treasure. Then the short one with the limp answered that they would go to Ponce tomorrow afternoon and look for it."

"Good night!" Pete whistled. "Can you tell us anything more?"

"No," Raul answered, as he removed his white apron.

"They're not the men we're looking for."

"Thanks," Carlos said. "You've been a great help to us."

As he and Pete joined the other children, everyone felt relieved that Stilts and Umberto were not going to Ponce immediately to hunt for the treasure.

Pam's eyes brightened. "That'll give us time to hunt for the missing guitar before we go!"

"Good idea," Maya said admiringly. "The instrument is worth more to Manuel than any treasure."

"Say," said Pete, "where is *Avenida de Diego*?"

"In Santurce," Carlos replied. "Why?"

Pete told of the store clerk in Shoreham who was a nephew of Mr. Pino who owned a music shop on the *Avenido*. "We promised to call on him and maybe he can help us find the guitar."

"You mean Stilts might have sold it to a music store?" Holly questioned.

"Yes."

Carlos knew where the store was and quickly directed Mr. Hollister to it. The children trouped inside. Many kinds of instruments were on display, including maracas and guayos.

"Are you Mr. Pino?" Pete asked, walking up to a friendly looking shopkeeper.

When the man said yes, Pete said he brought greetings from Enrique Pino in Shoreham.

"Ah! You know my nephew!" the shopkeeper exclaimed.

The Hollisters introduced themselves and the Villamil children. Mr. Pino said he was very pleased to hear news of his relative on the mainland.

"Now can I do something for you?" he asked, after they had chatted a few minutes.

"Perhaps you can," Pam said, and quickly told him the story of the stolen guitar.

"Where do you think we might find it?" Carlos asked.

Mr. Pino was silent several seconds, then replied, "My instruments are all new, but there is a shop in old San Juan which sells nothing but secondhand guitars. You might go there and look."

He scribbled the address on a piece of paper, saying it was near *Plaza Colon,* and gave it to Pete. who thanked him. Then the children said good-by. Mr. Pino sent a return message to his nephew and waved to them as they climbed into the car.

As Carlos directed Mr. Hollister along the waterfront, the visitors were intrigued by the blue sea and the great breakers which boomed upon the beach at the foot of the bluff to their right. When they reached *Plaza Colon,* Carlos suggested they park and and walk the rest of the way.

"The secondhand guitar shop is not far from here," he said. "Follow me."

By now the Hollisters were used to the narrow streets of the old city. In single file they hurried along the sidewalk after their Puerto Rican friends.

"Here's the place," Carlos said presently, as he

stopped before a grimy shopwindow. Back of it hung rows of secondhand guitars.

The children peered through the open doorway. It was cool and dim inside. At the far end of the store stood a counter with a thin little man seated on a stool behind it. They walked up to him.

"Good guitars for Americans," he said, with a smile which showed one front tooth missing and another made of gold.

"We're looking for a very special instrument," Pam said. "Did anyone sell a guitar to you yesterday or today?"

"Why do you want to know?"

Pete told him their story. When he finished, the shopkeeper said, "*Si si,* a tall man did sell me a guitar. *Caramba,* it was so beautiful! You say it was stolen?" He looked very worried.

"We want it back to give to Manuel," Holly spoke up.

"Oh, I wish I could do that," the man said, "but I do not have the guitar any more."

CHAPTER 12

THE OXEN LOCOMOTIVE

"You sold the guitar?" Pam asked, disappointed.

"*Si, si,* but I have the buyer's name and address. You may be able to get it from him."

The shopkeeper bustled into the back room and returned with a book. Turning to the last page written upon, he ran his finger across a line of writing. Then he said, "Mr. Targa bought that guitar."

"Does he live in San Juan?" Carlos asked.

The shopkeeper shook his head. "No, he lives in Ponce. Here's the address." He wrote it on a small business card and handed it to Carlos.

"Now we have two good reasons for going to Ponce," Pam said, as they thanked the man and left the shop.

"But maybe Mr. Targa won't give us the guitar," Holly said, worried.

"We can explain everything to him," Pam said. "After all, the guitar was stolen from Manuel."

"Let's go to the school for the blind right now," Pete said, "and tell Manuel about our clue."

Mr. Hollister quickly drove them to the place,

where they found Manuel and his friend Desi seated on a bench in the quadrangle.

"Hi!" cried the Hollisters and the Villamil children.

Greeting them in return, the blind boys squeezed the hands of their visitors and asked at once how they had made out with their detective work.

"All right so far," Pete replied, and told them the shopkeeper's story.

"Then you are going to Ponce?" Desi asked.

"Tomorrow morning," Pam said.

"Oh, I wish—I wish——" Manuel said, embarrassed.

"You wish you could come with us?" Pete said quickly.

"*Si, si.*"

"Then please do!" Pam said kindly.

"Sure, there'll be room enough for all of us," Pete added.

Desi was to have a special examination in English and could not leave. But he was happy that Manuel could make the trip to the south coast of the island.

"We'll call for you at eight in the morning, Manuel," Pam told him. Then they all said good-by.

That evening the children packed a few clothes for the trip in case they should stay overnight on the treasure hunt. While they were doing this, Mrs. Villamil planned a picnic lunch.

Next morning a hamper containing it was put into the car and the eager travelers gathered for the trip.

It was decided that Sue would stay with her mother and Mrs. Villamil, who had planned a shopping trip in San Juan.

"Good-by, Mother," Pam said, giving Mrs. Hollister a hug. "We're going to beat Stilts and Umberto to the treasure!"

Mrs. Hollister bent down to kiss Holly and the others. "Good luck to my young detectives," she said, as they climbed into the car.

Mr. Hollister drove the station wagon to the school for the blind, where Manuel was waiting near the entrance. He carried a small bag of clothes. The boy stepped aboard and sat down in the front seat.

"We're off to find the treasure," Pete said.

"And your guitar," Maya added.

"That makes me very happy," Manuel said.

Mr. Hollister followed highway number 1. It led south from San Juan, up and down beautiful green hills. Little farms stretched up the terraced slopes and Maya pointed out fields of tobacco. Along the roadside were banana trees.

"Oh, the bunches are growing upside down," Holly said.

Carlos explained that the tiny bananas hung down from their stems until they became so heavy the branch bent over.

"Then they look as if they're growing upside down," he said.

"I'm so glad you came during *zafra!*" Maya spoke up presently.

"Is that something like a zebra?" Ricky asked.

The Villamil children laughed. "No, *zafra* is the sugar-cane harvest," Maya said. "At that time everybody in Puerto Rico is happy because there's work for so many of our people."

A few miles farther on Mr. Hollister stopped beside one of the sugar-cane fields. Men were busy swinging long knives.

"They're cutting the cane with machetes," Carlos said.

Everyone except Manuel got out of the car and went down a little embankment to watch the men. They wore straw hats and work clothes. Their faces were tanned a ruddy brown.

Swish-swack went the machetes. The stalks toppled to the ground with every stroke.

"The cane looks like a cross between bamboo and corn," Pete remarked, squinting his eyes against the blazing sun.

Just then a short, bandy-legged man walked up to them and spoke to Carlos in Spanish. After a short conversation the boy turned to his friends.

"The foreman says, 'Would you boys like to try cutting sugar cane?' "

"Oh yes," Ricky and Pete said with enthusiasm.

"And I would too," Mr. Hollister said, grinning.

The foreman called to some of the workers. They stopped swinging their machetes and walked over to the Hollisters, smiling broadly, and handed their blades over to the visitors. Carlos warned them to be very careful of the sharp edges.

"Here's a place where you can cut," he said walking over to a section indicated by the foreman.

"Wow, this machete is sharp!" Pete said, as he cut several stalks of cane.

In a moment Maya said to the girls, "Would you like to taste the sugar cane?"

"Sure. How do you do that?" Holly asked.

The foreman took his knife and cut the cane into small lengths. He handed each of the Hollisters one of the pieces which were oozing at the ends with liquid.

The children sucked on the sugar cane. "Umm, it's good," Holly said. "It tastes something like maple sugar."

"And molasses too," Pam remarked.

The workers laughed and nodded as they watched the children enjoy the *caña,* as they called it.

"Look over there," Carlos said.

In the distance were two large oxen pulling a string of small cars which were loaded high with sugar cane.

"The cars are on narrow tracks," Maya said, "and the animals walk on either side of them."

"You mean the oxen are like locomotives?" Ricky asked with a grin. "Let's get closer and watch them."

Mr. Hollister and the children hurried over and watched as the oxen strained forward while the driver prodded them with a long stick.

127

"Um, this sugar cane is good."

"I'm going on the other side of the tracks for a better look," Ricky called out, and ran in front of the beasts.

As he reached the far rail, his right shoe stubbed against the track. He fell flat on his face in front of one of the lunging oxen!

"Look out!" Pam shrieked, horrified.

The ox driver did not see what had happened. He kept urging the beasts toward the stunned boy!

The one ox was almost upon Ricky when Mr. Hollister dashed forward and snatched his son out of the way!

"*Caramba!*" the driver exclaimed, now aware of what had happened.

"That was a close one!" Carlos said, as everyone ran up to Ricky.

"I'm okay," he said. "But I'll never run in front of an ox train again!"

Pete told his father they ought to leave. "We'd better hurry to get to Ponce before Stilts and Umberto."

"That's right."

Getting into the car, Pam noticed a motorcycle parked on the road behind them. It had not been there when they arrived. She mentioned this to Carlos.

"It probably belongs to a workman," he said. "Many of them ride motorcycles."

Once on the road again Pam suggested that they

eat their lunch while driving. "It will save us more time for treasure hunting," she said.

Ricky agreed noisily and Holly told Maya, "He's always hungry. Mother says he has a hollow leg."

After the girls had helped themselves to plump chicken sandwiches, Ricky set about to prove both legs were hollow!

Not long after the lunch was finished, they came to the outskirts of Ponce. Mr. Hollister pulled into a gasoline station to ask directions to Mr. Targa's home.

"He lives on Cristobal Street," the young attendant said, and gave directions.

A few minutes later the station wagon reached a narrow street flanked on both sides by neat, one-story buildings. Mr. Hollister stopped it in front of one which was painted white and yellow.

Pete got out and rapped on the door. It was opened by a sweet-faced, white-haired woman.

"Are you Mrs. Targa?" he asked.

"*Si.*"

"May we speak to your husband?"

"He is working at the *central.*"

"Does he have a new guitar?" Pete continued.

"*Si*, a beautiful one," the woman replied with a questioning look. "He has it with him."

Pete thanked her and they drove out of town toward the sugar mill. The road to it was narrow and twisting.

"What's that up ahead?" Pam asked Maya as the station wagon wound around a curve.

"A sugar-cane truck."

All that could be seen were two back wheels, above which was a very tall load of cane. The truck sped along the road, swaying from side to side, its horn being blown constantly.

"That driver should not go so fast," Carlos said. "The load is top heavy. It may fall over."

The truck continued to sway dangerously, roaring around the bends.

Suddenly Pam screamed, "Look!"

The careening truck hit a rut in the side of the road. It teetered wildly and toppled over!

CHAPTER 13

BLACK SUGAR

As THE sugar-cane truck toppled to the side of the road the children gasped. Mr. Hollister stopped the station wagon and they all got out.

"I hope nobody is hurt!" Pam said.

They ran forward to where the truck lay on its side, one of its back wheels still spinning. The cane was strewn across the road and the children had to climb through it to get to the truck.

The driver, who apparently had been alone, lay on the pavement beside the vehicle. He was a slender young fellow.

Pete was the first to reach him. Bending down, the boy observed that the man was still breathing.

"I think he's just knocked out, Dad," Pete said as Mr. Hollister knelt beside the driver.

Pam chafed the fellow's wrists while Pete massaged the back of his neck. The Puerto Rican began to stir. He opened his eyes and looked up at the group gathered around him.

"*Que pasa?*" he said.

"That means 'What's going on?'" Carlos trans-

133

lated. "Your truck turned over," he told the man. "You were going very fast."

The driver rose to his feet shakily and asked Carlos several questions in Spanish.

"Doesn't he speak English?" Holly asked.

Maya told her that the driver came from the interior and knew only a little English.

"Me Rafael. I ahm lokey," the driver said with a wry smile.

Holly remarked that she did not think he was so lucky. Half of the sugar cane had spilled out of the overturned truck.

Just then a horn sounded down the road. Another car wanted to pass. Immediately the boys pitched in to lift the heaps of sugar cane to the side of the road.

Meanwhile, Rafael spoke to the native occupants of the car, asking them to send a wrecker back from the next village. They promised to do this and drove on.

When the Hollisters were certain that Rafael was not injured they said good-by and continued toward the *central*.

"See you later, alligator," Ricky said impishly.

Carlos chuckled and said, *"Hasta luego, logarto."*

"What did you say?" Pam asked.

"The same thing, only in Spanish," Carlos replied, grinning.

After going up one steep hill and down another the road burst out of a canopy of dense foliage into a broad plain. On either side of the road were thousands of acres of sugar cane.

"There's the *central*," Maya said as she pointed to what looked like a factory in the distance.

It reminded Pete of a steel mill with a tall smokestack and corrugated-metal roof. Mr. Hollister turned into a side road. As they neared the *central*, trucks loaded with sugar cane appeared from the fields. Finally they came to a whole line of trucks parked at the side of the road, awaiting their turn to enter the *central*. The drivers waved and grinned at the children as the station wagon passed them.

"Oh, what a sweet smell!" Holly said as they drove up alongside the sugar mill.

"That's the juice from the cane," Maya told her.

Manuel, who had sat quietly for most of the trip, smiled when he noticed the wonderful aroma. "It reminds me of the town where I live," he said. "We have a *central* there."

Carlos suggested that Mr. Hollister drive up to the main office. "If we tell the manager we would like to visit the mill, I'm sure he will be glad to show us through it."

Mr. Hollister pulled up in front of a low building across the street from the sugar mill. Several workers were lounging about the steps. One of the older men was seated on the ground, his back against the wall. He held a guitar. As the children stepped from the car, he began to strum a tune.

Manuel stopped and listened. "The name of that is 'Little Boy in the Sugar Cane Field,'" he said.

The musician smiled and nodded. He was a pleasant, middle-aged man, rather stout and possessing a jolly smile. Learning that the children liked the music, he played louder, his brown fingers dancing over the strings of the guitar.

As Mr. Hollister mounted the steps to enter the office, he noticed a queer expression come over Manuel's face.

"What's the matter?" he asked. "Don't you feel well?"

At first the boy stood still, listening intently to the guitar. "I feel well. But I am sure that is my guitar!" the blind boy said softly.

The Hollisters and the Villamils looked at Manuel, surprised. "Your stolen guitar?" Pam whispered.

"Yes. I can tell by the sweetness of the tone," Manuel said. "There was no other guitar like mine. But look for a white star on the back of it."

The musician was playing so loudly that he did not overhear the conversation. "Do you suppose that's Mr. Targa?" Pete said.

"Let's ask him," Maya suggested.

With Mr. Hollister looking on intently, the children waited for the man to finish his song. Then Pete stepped up to him and said, "We enjoyed it very much. Are you Mr. Targa?"

The musician looked up in surprise. "*Si, si.* But I can't understand how you knew."

136

"That is my guitar!"

"It's quite a story," Mr. Hollister said. "You'd better tell him all about it, Pete."

Introductions were quickly made. Then Pete told Mr. Targa the tale of the stolen guitar and pointed out the star identification.

"*Si.* I did buy it in San Juan," the man said, "and if it belongs to Manuel, he shall have it back." He handed the instrument to the boy.

Manuel was overjoyed to receive the guitar. He caressed it fondly. *"Gracias, gracias, señor,"* he said. "What can I do to repay you?"

Mr. Targa smiled. "Make happy music," he said. "The joy you give to others will be my payment."

"You are a very kind man," Pam said, "but you shouldn't lose the money you paid for the guitar."

Mr. Targa said he would go to San Juan again in a few days. "I will try to get my money back from the shopkeeper," he said. "But don't worry about that."

The man explained that the *siesta*—the rest period—was now over. He must return to his job in the mill. He tended the rollers that pressed the juice from the sugar cane.

"May we see how the rollers work?" Pete asked.

Mr. Targa said he thought it could be arranged. He took them into the office and introduced everyone to the *central* manager, a stocky, mustached man named Mr. Oro.

"Yes, of course, we will be happy to have you visit our *central*," he said. Then, turning to Mr.

138

Targa, he added, "I will have somebody take your place at the rollers. You show our guests around."

Pam took Manuel by the hand, as everyone followed Mr. Targa out of the office.

"Sugar cane is ground twenty-four hours a day for six days," he said. "Then the *central* rests on Sunday."

The first thing he showed the children was how huge cranes lifted the cane from the trucks high into the air, then let the stalks fall into a chute.

"Now come with me and be careful," Mr. Targa said as he led them inside the building.

Here the cane was carried along a trough on a conveyor belt. Next it passed through a series of choppers, which cut the stalks into small pieces.

Mr. Targa led the visitors up a little stairway to a long platform. On the left of it were the huge rollers. On the right, in a deep pit, was the machinery used to run the mill. A big flywheel turned around slowly.

"Boy, oh boy!" Ricky said. "That's the largest wheel I ever saw."

"But look over here," Pam said.

The cane was fed through one set of rollers after another. As the chopped-up sugar cane was squeezed between the giant rollers, the juice spilled down into a large pan directly beneath.

"Where does it go now?" Pete shouted above the sound of the machinery.

"Come this way and I'll show you," their guide said.

The visitors descended another flight of iron stairs and Mr. Targa led them before a row of immense kettles. Alongside these stood workmen stripped to the waist.

"Phew! It's hot in here!" Holly said, tossing back her pigtails.

"It has to be," Carlos said. "Watch what happens."

Into the large kettles came a stream of sugar juice. Then the kettles began to revolve rapidly.

Mr. Targa bent close to Pam's ear. "The heat and the spinning granulate the sugar," he said.

When the kettle stopped spinning, the brown mass inside was no longer juice. It was brown sugar. This was shoveled out of the container and put on a conveyer belt.

"Black sugar, we call it in Puerto Rico," Carlos said, as they followed the path of the sweet stuff.

"The next step is bagging," Mr. Targa said, pointing to a platform where the sugar was being fed into large sacks. When two hundred fifty pounds of black sugar fell into a sack, it was automatically moved off that platform and sewn by a stitching machine. Then the bags were dropped onto another conveyer belt.

"Now they're ready to be stacked," Mr. Targa said.

As Ricky passed a wooden post he looked up. There were three buttons on a control panel. The others walked along, but not Ricky. Buttons in-

140

trigued him. "I wonder what would happen," he said to himself, "if I pressed one."

Ricky could not resist an impulse to find out. Quickly looking about, he pressed one of the buttons. The noise in the conveyer belt suddenly stopped.

"Oh, oh," Ricky said to himself. Look what I did."

He knew he was in trouble. Which of the other two buttons should he push to start the belt again? Before the boy had time to decide, something else was happening. Bags of sugar which were weighed and stitched now had no place to go. They dropped onto the stationary conveyer belt, falling this way and that.

Suddenly a man's voice cried out. Several workmen ran to where Ricky was standing. The confusion caused Mr. Targa and his guests to turn about. They all hurried toward Ricky.

"What did you do?" the man asked excitedly.

"I—I just pushed this button," Ricky said.

Mr. Targa quickly pressed the one above it. The conveyer belt started again while several workmen piled the toppled sugar bags in their proper places.

Ricky hung his head as he followed the others to watch the end of the conveyer belt. Here the sacks toppled onto handcarts held by waiting workmen and were pushed off to one end of the big building to be stacked into high piles.

As the other children chattered, Ricky appeared glum over what he had done. Noticing this Mr.

Targa put his arm about the boy's shoulders and whispered, "Don't worry, *muchacho*, you're not the first one to do this. I tried it once when I was a little boy!"

This pleased Ricky and he grinned as the visitors filed out of the sugar mill. Mr. Targa led his party to the shade of a flamboyant tree.

"Now, are there any other questions you would like to ask me?" he said, as they sat on the grass to cool off.

"I have a question, but not about sugar," Holly said.

"What is it?"

"Are there any pirates around here?"

Mr. Targa laughed heartily. "Not nowadays," he said. "But in the olden days Puerto Rico was a favorite place for pirates. In fact, Ponce, where I live, was built back from the coast so that pirate ships could not attack it."

It suddenly occurred to Pete that perhaps Mr. Targa could give them information about their treasure hunt.

"Have you ever heard of the legend of the princess's emerald crown?" he asked.

The man gave him an expansive smile. "*Si, si,*" he said. "I can tell you something about the Green Pirate."

CHAPTER 14

SEASHORE SEARCH

"You know about the Green Pirate?" Pam asked Mr. Targa excitedly as she held Holly's hand.

The man nodded. "It's an old legend," he answered, "and may not be true. But the Green Pirate was believed to have raided the town of Ponce two hundred years ago."

"Do you know anything about the emerald crown?" Maya asked, thinking perhaps Mr. Targa knew more of the legend than her father did.

The man looked thoughtful for a moment as if searching his memory. "When I was a boy," he said finally, "my grandfather told me that the Green Pirate had buried a treasure somewhere inland. The hiding place was indicated by directions cut into several stone markers."

The children's hearts raced at this news. Pam

squeezed Holly's hand as a signal not to tell of their wonderful clue. Pete gave Ricky a cautious wink.

"Has anyone found the markers?" Pete asked.

"No, they have not," Mr. Targa said. "Treasure hunters have been looking for years with no success."

Pam felt as if she would burst with excitement. Of all the mysteries the children had worked on, this was perhaps the most thrilling! One of the secret stone markers already had been found. Now if they could only locate the second clue left by the Green Pirate!

The young sleuths could hardly wait to get started. Eagerness showed in every face, and Mr. Hollister's as well.

Everyone thanked Mr. Targa for his courtesy. Before leaving, Mr. Hollister shook hands with him and promised to help get the guitar money refunded.

Before Manuel stepped into the station wagon he gave Mr. Targa a grateful hug. "I'll always remember your kindness," he said.

Once everyone was seated inside the car, the children waved good-by and they started for Ponce. Immediately Pete told Manuel their part of the secret. Then he began to speculate upon where a second marker might have been left by the Green Pirate. Pam said she thought the beach would be the most natural place.

"But Ponce is not on the ocean," Pete reminded her.

"The town does have a harbor," Maya said.

"That's right," Manuel added. "It's called *Playa de Ponce.*"

Carlos said the place was not far from Ponce and asked if they might drive there.

"Of course," Mr. Hollister said, chuckling. "With the luck you young detectives have, I wouldn't be surprised if I leave this town with an emerald crown."

"Oh, Daddy, you'd look funny wearing it," Holly said, giggling.

"Maybe I'd look better with a pineapple crown," her father joked as they drove along.

Not long afterward he passed through Ponce and turned toward the harbor. It was midafternoon by the time they arrived at the beach.

"I hope we got here before Stilts and Umberto," said Pam, looking around.

No one was in sight—it was *siesta* time for many people.

"Phew! I'm hot!" Holly said. "Let's all get wet!"

"If you wish to romp in the surf," her father replied, I'll leave you here while I go to have the car checked for gas and oil."

"Okay, Dad," Pete said. "I'll take care of things."

They all got out of the car, with Manuel carefully carrying his precious guitar. Pam led him to a palm tree, where he sat down on a grassy mound. Then as the lilting strains of Spanish music filled the air, the other children removed their shoes and socks and raced along the white surf which foamed over the smooth sand.

"Pam, look out!"

After a few minutes of scampering about Maya suddenly screamed, "Pam, look out!"

"What's the matter?"

"A jellyfish!"

Pam glanced down at the sand where Maya was pointing. A blobby, transparent mass lay there near her left foot. Pam leaped out of the sea creature's way as Maya said excitedly:

"It nearly stung you!"

The next wave dashed the jellyfish up on the sand, where Carlos covered it with a stone.

"If there are jellyfish in the area we'd better stay out of the water," Carlos warned.

"Yes," said Maya. "And let's find the second marker."

Ricky put his hand to his chin and stood deep in thought.

"The wheels are going round in his head," Pam said jokingly. "What are you trying to figure out, Ricky?"

The freckled-faced boy wrinkled his nose and replied, "What would I have done if I had been the Green Pirate?"

"Cut off somebody's head, I guess," Holly said with a giggle.

"No, I mean where would I have hidden the second marker?"

"Your guess is as good as mine," said Pam.

As they started off along the beach, Pete thought

147

the buccaneer would have made the second marker to look the same as the first.

"Then shall we look for a stone tower?" Maya asked.

"That's a good idea," Carlos declared. "It might be located among the trees fringing the shore."

Leaving Manuel still playing his guitar, the others walked farther and farther up the curving shore, looking for an object resembling a stone marker. The beach was deserted. This pleased the children.

After they had walked for half an hour without finding the marker, Holly flopped down on the sand. "Pete," she said, "the tower must have been knocked down long ago."

Carlos was inclined to agree. "I didn't think we'd be lucky enough to find both markers," he said with a sigh. "Let's go back."

Pete glanced across the sand, which was shimmering in the heat. Good detectives, he remembered, never gave up. He looked at Pam. "What do you say, sis?"

"Let's go on a little farther."

"Okay," Pete scooped up some cool water and washed his face. The others did the same.

"Now that we all feel cool," Maya said, smiling, "we'll go on with the search."

After another ten minutes of determined trudging they saw nothing on the shore that in any way resembled the stone tower on the Villamil property.

"Pete, I don't think we should leave Manuel alone

any longer," Pam said finally. "Besides Dad might have returned by now and be worried about us. We've been gone a long time."

"I guess you're right," Pete said in a discouraged tone. "We'll go back."

It was a long hot trek to the place from which they had started. Nearing the spot, the weary children saw two figures. One was waving at them wildly.

"It's Dad!" Pete cried out.

"He's awfully excited about something," Holly said, as they all dashed across the sand.

Mr. Hollister took the blind boy's hand and hurried to meet the others.

"What's the matter?" Ricky called out, cupping his hands.

"We've found it!" Mr. Hollister shouted, his face flushed with excitement.

The children were dumfounded for a moment. Pete was the first to speak. "You found the stone marker, Dad?"

"Yes. Manuel got a clue to it when he felt a sharp stone jutting out from the mound on which he was sitting."

"Crickets!" yelled Pete.

Mr. Hollister led the children to the spot. "Apparently the tower was knocked down many years ago and earth accumulated over the rubble."

"Except that one of the stones stuck out," Manuel said.

By using a jack handle, a hammer, and a screw driver from the car's toolkit, Mr. Hollister had already unearthed several of the stones. They were the same size and shape as the ones on the Villamil property.

"What luck Manuel brought us!" Ricky exclaimed, as everybody started to dig into the mound.

Stone after stone was removed, taken to the surf to be washed off, and examined. But after thirty stones had been handled in this way, no writing could be found.

When nearly all the slabs had been dug out Holly said suddenly, "Who's that man over there?"

"Where?" Pete asked.

The girl pointed to a grove of trees some distance from the mound of stones. "He's gone now," she added.

"Maybe it was Stilts or Umberto!" Carlos said uneasily.

"We'll have to keep our eyes open for them," Pete warned as they prepared to take the last of the stones to the surf bath.

He lugged a heavy one to the water's edge and rubbed off the soil which clung to it. Seven sides were smooth. The eighth face was rough!

With a whoop of delight, Pete ran to show it to the others. But when the sun dried the surface, there was only the faintest sign of writing.

"I'm afraid even a plaster mold wouldn't show this up," Mr. Hollister said sadly.

"Oh dear, our mystery has come to an end!" Pam declared with a sigh.

CHAPTER 15

THE CHASE

"No ONE will ever be able to decipher the message," Pete moaned as he ran his hand over the face of the aged stone.

Even Mr. Hollister felt certain that the wind, sand, and water had cut so much of the surface away that the writing was illegible.

Suddenly Pam's face brightened. She called to Manuel who was seated on the sand, "Is it true that blind people have very sensitive fingers?"

"Yes," the boy replied. "It is because we have to depend so much on our sense of touch."

"Then maybe you can figure out the message," she said, taking him by the hand and leading him to where the stone lay on the beach.

Manuel bent over it, his long slender fingers moving back and forth across the faint indentations. As the others watched breathlessly, a smile played over the boy's lips.

"The message is in Spanish," he said, "and I am reading it."

"You're wonderful!" Pam exclaimed.

"What does it say?" Mr. Hollister asked eagerly.

The blind boy ran his fingers over the face of the stone several times more then began to speak slowly:

"It says: The crown of the Infanta is buried on the top of Sugar Loaf Hill near the *Rio Grande de Manati*. It lies under a flat white rock."

Mr. Hollister and the children, spellbound while the blind boy translated the message, now broke into excited cheers.

"Hurray, hurray!" Holly cried out and jumped up and down in the sand.

"We've solved the ancient mystery!" Ricky shouted.

"Sh! Not so loud!" Maya warned.

As they quieted down, Pete said, "We haven't solved it yet. There's still a lot of searching to do. Say, Manati is where the pineapples grow isn't it?"

"Yes," Pam agreed. "Remember Mr. Sifre whose copter crashed near the beach? He lives there."

"Maybe the treasure is near his plantation!" Ricky suggested.

Just then they heard someone cough behind a large bougainvillea bush at the rear of the beach. The Hollisters whirled about, Pete and Ricky dashing for the spot. As they neared the bush, a man jumped out of hiding and raced off.

"Stop!" Pete cried out.

The fellow darted into a palm-tree grove, but not before Ricky caught a glimpse of his face.

"Stilts!" he yelled. "After him, everybody!"

154

"Stop!" Pete cried.

Hearing this, Mr. Hollister dashed across the sand but in his haste lost one of his shoes. By the time he had put it back on the children were far ahead of him. Pete was in the lead, followed by Ricky and Carlos.

The fugitive, dodging this way and that, threw them off his trail several times, but his white shirt was easy to detect against the green background of the shrubs.

"We're gaining on him!" Pete cried, as the barefooted boys raced down a path which led to the highway.

By this time Mr. Hollister and the girls were so far behind that they could not be seen.

"We still have a chance to catch Stilts!" Carlos cried out.

The fugitive was becoming winded. Gasping for breath, he dragged himself across the last few yards onto the highway. He headed for a motorcycle parked on the roadside. Reaching it, he flung himself into the seat, started the machine, and roared off.

Pete, who was closest, made a lunge for the machine, barely missing the back seat. Tears of anger came to the boy's eyes as the rider sped off down the highway.

"Stilts knows our secret!" he moaned. "He may get to Sugar Loaf Hill before we do."

Carlos suggested that Mr. Hollister chase Stilts in the station wagon.

"We can try but I'm afraid we'd be too late," Pete said. "Those motorcycles go fast!"

Ricky suggested that they follow the tire tracks, but, once they had examined the road, they realized this would be impossible. There were several tire marks visible on the surface. To follow them closely would be far too time-consuming.

"Let's talk to your father about it," Carlos urged, and they quickly retraced their steps along the wooded path.

Presently they could hear the voices of the others approaching them in the distance.

"I hate to tell them the bad news," Pete said. "If only——"

Suddenly Carlos, who was walking behind him, gave Pete a terrific shove. The boy sprawled head over heels and sat on the ground, looking up in surprise.

"Why did you do that, Carlos?" he asked, picking himself up.

"I'm sorry, but you nearly stepped on a spider," the Puerto Rican boy said. "Come here, look!"

Beside the path, partly concealed by a fallen palm frond was a large, dangerous-looking, black spider. Carlos explained that there were only a few poisonous creatures on the island. The black spider was one of them.

"Yikes, you just missed him," Ricky burst out.

"Thanks to you, Carlos," Pete said gratefully. "I'd sure hate to be bitten."

Just then the girls came along the trail with Mr. Hollister. When they heard the story of Stilt's escape, all looked disappointed. Pete's father agreed with him that a chase now would probably be futile.

"Then what do we do now?" Holly asked.

It was agreed they should go back to the beach where they had left Manuel and hold a conference. They found the blind boy strumming on his guitar and the lovely native music made them feel more relaxed.

When Manuel stopped playing, Pete told him what had happened. Then the group sprawled on the sand and talked about what to do next.

"To find the right sugar-loaf hill will be very difficult," Maya remarked. "There are hundreds of that type near Manati."

"Yes," her brother agreed. "But Stilts will have trouble, too, even if he did overhear our conversation."

"It might take us weeks to locate the right hill," Mr. Hollister said, "if we try to search each one."

"And we're only going to be here for a short time," Pam said with a sigh.

Pete looked thoughtful. "I suppose we could use an airplane," he said, "but where could we get one?"

Pam's tanned face lighted up. "How about Mr. Sifre's copter?" she asked. "He said he'd like to do us a favor."

"Terrific! Let's ask him!" Pete urged eagerly.

The prospect of a search for the emerald crown by helicopter pleased all the young treasure hunters.

"Where do you suppose we can find Señor Sifre?" Maya asked.

"Let's try calling his cannery at Manati," Pam said.

Mr. Hollister agreed this was a good idea. "Who wants to make the call?" he asked.

Since Pam had thought of the plan for Señor Sifre's help, the other children decided that she should be the one to place the telephone call.

The children got into the station wagon again and Mr. Hollister drove back along the road to Ponce until they came to a drugstore which had a telephone booth. Pam quickly got the operator, who connected her with Manati. In a few minutes she had Señor Sifre on the wire.

The other children standing outside the booth watched Pam's expression intently. They could see that she was explaining the situation and when her face broke into a wide smile they knew she had been successful in her request.

Pam hung up and opened the door. "He's coming, he's coming!" she cried gleefully.

CHAPTER 16

AN UNFRIENDLY PLANE

"How soon can Mr. Sifre come with his copter?" Ricky cried out excitedly. "I can't wait to find that princess's crown!"

"Mr. Sifre will meet us at the Ponce airport to-morrow morning at nine," Pam reported.

"Goody! Goody!" Holly exclaimed. "Oh, Daddy, may we stay here overnight?"

"I'll call the Villamil house and find out if it will be all right," he said.

After talking with Mrs. Hollister at Lizard Cove, he told the children they would stay and drove the young people to a hotel in Ponce. Once supper was over, everyone went to bed early, tired from their exciting day and eager to be up early.

At quarter to nine the next morning they were gathered at the airport awaiting the arrival of Señor Sifre. Pete kept glancing at his wrist watch. At two minutes of nine he exclaimed:

"Here he comes!"

In the distance the helicopter looked like a black

bug whirring down toward the airfield, its rotors glistening in the morning sun. When the craft landed, the Hollisters and their friends rushed over to it.

As the motor stopped and the giant blades whispered to a standstill, the door opened and Señor Sifre stepped out. Grinning, he hurried over to shake hands with everybody.

"My pilot and I got here as quickly as possible," he said. "We are happy to return the favor you did for us."

Ken Jones hopped out of the cockpit and said, "Second the motion!"

"I understand there is a big mystery connected with the flight we are about to make," Señor Sifre said, smiling.

"Yes," Carlos replied, and quickly related what had happened. "We must locate the hill with the white marker and get there before Stilts and Umberto do, or they may discover the emerald crown."

Ken Jones chuckled. "We'll call this 'Operation Emerald,'" he said, "and there are eight of you—*si?*"

Mr. Hollister said at once he would not go. Instead he would drive to Manati and meet them there.

Carlos spoke up. "The Hollisters are better detectives than Maya and me. We'll drive back with Mr. Hollister and take Manuel with us."

Pete objected, saying that if they found the treasure, it should go to the Villamils.

The pilot suddenly smiled broadly. "This copter

doesn't care how many people it carries so long as the weight isn't more than that of six men. Now suppose you all tell me how much you weigh."

Eagerly the children told him and he added the figures. He smiled. "If Mr. Hollister wants to take Manuel with him to Manati, the rest of you can go."

"Swell!" Pete cried out.

Waving good-by to Mr. Hollister and Manuel, the children climbed the steps into the helicopter. The door was closed. Señor Sifre took his place beside Ken Jones in the cockpit. Holly was on Pam's lap and Ricky on Pete's.

"Here we go!" Carlos shouted.

The motor started with a roar and the two sets of blades began to spin. Faster and faster they went, and the helicopter slowly lifted. Then Ken Jones dipped the nose of the helicopter and it sped northward over the lush countryside of valleys and mountains toward the north coast.

"I wonder how fast we're going," Pam said.

Pete called up to Señor Sifre and repeated the question.

"A hundred miles an hour," came the reply. "We'll be in the Manati area before long."

Twenty minutes later a snaking river appeared below them. "That's the Manati River!" Ken Jones called out. "Now we'll go downstairs for a better look at the sugar-loaf hills."

The helicopter soon was flying about fifty feet above the knobby green hills. The boys looked out of one side of the craft while the girls scanned the view from the opposite window. Hill after hill passed beneath the helicopter, but no white marker was visible. The pilot slowly went up one side of the river and then down the other. The sugar-loaf mounds all looked the same, covered with dense foliage and an occasional palm tree.

Finally Señor Sifre turned about in his seat. "We'll have to land to pick up more gas," he said, "but we'll go right back on the search again."

Heading off to the northeast, the helicopter soon was hovering over a huge pineapple plantation. Near the edge of it stood a long one-story building.

"That's our cannery," Señor Sifre said. "We'll land alongside it."

The plane became stationary, then eased straight down into a small field. When the motor stopped, everybody got out. Ken Jones walked rapidly to a gasoline pump nearby and pulled a long hose from it so that he might refuel the aircraft.

Señor Sifre, meanwhile, led the Hollisters among the growing pineapples. He pointed out that the fruit grows out of the center of a cactuslike plant.

"There are two main varieties," he explained. "The smooth Cayenne is grown mainly in Hawaii and has smooth stalks. But here we raise the Spanish red pineapple. They have prickly leaves. Watch out for them."

He led the children a short way into the field. Rows of pineapples were growing as far as the eye could see. Ricky bent over to smell one of them. Suddenly he exclaimed, "Ouch!"

"What happened?" Pam asked him.

"I—I backed into a pricker," the boy said. Señor Sifre chuckled and cautioned the children to beware of the spikes on the queen of fruits.

"Why do you call it the queen?" Pam asked.

"Because it's the only fruit that wears a crown," Señor Sifre replied. Then he guided them back to the cannery. "We'll have a few minutes before Ken is ready. I'll show you what we do here."

Outside the building and under an overhanging shed was a machine into which two workmen fed pineapples. On the other side the fruit came out hulled and cored.

"Now we'll look inside the cannery," Señor Sifre said.

Conveyer belts carried the pineapples to long tables at which stood women in white uniforms. Some of them cut the tiny eyes out, while others counted the pineapple rings and put them into cans.

Still other smiling women stuffed pineapple "fingers" into metal containers. Everybody worked rapidly and happily.

"I'd love to work here," said Ricky. "Then I could eat and eat and——"

"Get sick," Holly finished for him.

The children were ushered past a large vat containing pineapple juice. Señor Sifre poured some of it into paper cups and passed the juice to the chil-

"Ouch!"

dren. As they finished drinking it, Ken Jones beckoned Señor Sifre.

"We're ready to go," he said.

With a roar the helicopter took off again and soon Ken Jones was flying up and down the banks of the Manati River. Keeping their eyes fixed on the countryside below, the children scanned mound after mound but could see nothing resembling a white marker.

Suddenly Pete called out to the pilot. "Airplane at nine o'clock high." He had heard fliers say this on television shows. It meant directly to the left and above them.

"I see him," Ken replied. "A small four-seater."

As he said this, the airplane flew in their direction. It circled around the helicopter, coming closer and closer to it. Behind the pilot sat two men, peering out the windows.

Suddenly Pam cried out, "Stilts and Umberto!"

"Those are our enemies!" Holly told Señor Sifre and Ken Jones.

"Really?" said the pilot. "We'd better watch them closely."

Meanwhile Ricky was glancing first at the plane, then at the ground. "I just saw something white!" he exclaimed, pointing to the sugar loaf hill below them.

"Is it the marker?" Pam asked excitedly.

"I think it is!"

The others glanced down. But their attention

suddenly was diverted by the airplane. It bore down on them, its motor buzzing like an angry hornet.

"It's going to hit us!" Holly cried out fearfully.

CHAPTER 17

TREASURE MOUNTAIN

THE plane came so close to the helicopter that everyone was worried. Ken Jones quickly veered away.

"Maybe they've seen the white marker too," Ricky said, worried.

"I believe they're only trying to scare us so we'll leave," Señor Sifre said.

"But we're not going to let them, are we?" Holly asked.

"Indeed we're not," said the pilot.

At Pete's urging, Ken brought his craft down low over the hill to which Ricky had pointed. There was a small white patch among the green foliage.

"I think you've discovered the marker, Ricky," Pam said, hugging her brother.

"We'll have to go down for a good look at it," Señor Sifre said.

"Sorry, but that's not possible," Ken replied. "There's not enough space to land. the blades might clip a treetop."

Pete spoke up. "Have you a rope ladder, Ken?"

"Yes. It's in a locker under your feet."

Pete was nearly thrown off.

"Could you stand still in the air and let me down onto a tree?" the boy asked.

The pilot said he could, but Pete would have to be very careful.

"I can make it," the boy assured him. "Then I'll find out what that white spot is."

"I can't let you go alone," Señor Sifre said. "I'll follow you, Pete."

"And I will too," Carlos said with determination.

"But what'll we do about those ruffians in the other plane?" Ken said. "They may land in that valley over yonder and hike back to the hill."

Pam suggested that Ken fly to Manati and bring back the police.

"That's good advice," said Señor Sifre.

Ken Jones let the helicopter down nearly to tree-top level of a large leaning palm. Pete then launched the rope ladder over the side. Gripping it firmly, he made his way down, rung by rung.

As he grasped the last rung of the ladder, his feet touched the palm branches. He was just about to let go, when suddenly a gust of wind lifted the helicopter for several feet into the air.

"Hold on!" Pam screamed from above.

Pete's fingers tightened on the rope ladder just in time. He was nearly thrown off but maintained his grip as the helicopter lowered him again. This time the boy dropped safely into the palm branches and walked monkey-fashion down the sloping trunk.

"Here I come!" called Carlos.

His descent was smooth. Señor Sifre came last. When the three were safely on the ground, Ken headed in the direction of Manati.

Meanwhile the plane with Stilts and Umberto circled low over the spot where Pete, Carlos, and Señor Sifre had landed. The boys were worried but the older man reminded them that the plane could not land there.

"See? It is leaving already," he said.

Pete led the way through the dense foliage toward the spot where Ricky had spied the white object.

"Keep over to the left," Carlos called presently, then added, "We'll have to work fast in case those men do land and come to find us."

The top of the sugar-loaf hill was no larger than a football field. But the tropical growth was so thick that the white object was not easy to find on foot.

"I saw it so clearly from the plane," Pete said as they crisscrossed the area.

Beads of perspiration stood out on the searchers' foreheads as they walked laboriously through the high grass, pushing the bushes to left and right as they trekked along. Señor Sifre warned the boys to be wary of spiders.

"The marker must have been on the highest part of the knoll," Pete reasoned, "or otherwise it wouldn't be seen at all."

"The highest ground is over there," Señor Sifre said, pointing to a little ridge on the far side of the hill.

172

The trio made their way toward the spot and finally came near it. The trade winds had swept the area free of trees and only low bushes grew there.

"The white thing must be here," Pete declared as they reached the place.

The hot sun beat down on their heads as the three searchers began to crisscross the knoll. They kicked aside the low shrubs to get a better look at the ground itself.

Suddenly Pete cried out, "I see it!"

Carlos and Señor Sifre raced to the boy's side. He was bending over a three-foot square slab of marble. Only the center of it had been visible from the air. Now, as the searchers ripped the grassy fringe from about the marker, their excitement grew intense.

"We have found it! We have found the secret hiding place!" Carlos said in an excited whisper.

"If we can only lift the stone!" Señor Sifre said.

He tugged at the edges with his finger tips. The marble was only half an inch thick.

Pete examined the stone again. "I think if we all lift on one side," he said, "we may be able to budge it."

But they could not get a good grip on the heavy stone.

"Does either of you have a penknife?" Pete asked.

"I do," Carlos replied, pulling it from his pocket. "You want me to dig away some of the dirt so we can get our fingers under the stone?"

"Yes."

Carlos quickly scraped three separate places where their fingers could fit under the edge of the slab.

"Ready to lift?" he asked.

"Okay!" Pete replied.

"One—two—three!"

Straining with all their might, Señor Sifre and the boys lifted the marble several inches. Then, getting a better grip, they heaved it upright and flopped the stone over.

"Crickets, that sure was heavy!" Pete said, panting.

The ground beneath was dark and bare. The two boys quickly began digging in it, Pete with his fingers, Carlos with the penknife. Two inches underground they came upon the outline of a metal box.

"Here it is!" Pete exclaimed excitedly, hardly daring to believe their good fortune.

They brushed aside the loose soil, then Carlos got his hands around the metal container which was twice the size of a shoe box.

"Do you suppose this is really it?" he murmured.

Señor Sifre's eyes were wide with excitement as the boy lifted the box out. The metal was still sturdy.

"Open it, quick!" Pete whispered.

Carlos picked up the pocketknife and carefully began to pry off the lid. In a moment it fell back.

"What's the matter?" Señor Sifre asked, moving forward to take a look.

"There's nothing here," Carlos said in disappointment. He looked as if he might cry.

"Let me see it," Pete requested and Carlos stepped aside.

After examining the inside of the box, Pete said, "Let me have your knife, Carlos. I believe the box has a false bottom."

Hopefully Carlos handed over the knife and Pete slid it down the sides to loosen the bottom. In a few minutes the metal piece came free and the boy lifted it out.

Below lay a small golden crown beautifully studded with emeralds!

For a moment Señor Sifre and the boys stared openmouthed, hardly able to believe they had found the ancient treasure of Puerto Rico.

"The Infanta's crown!" Pete said with awe. "It's—it's——"

Suddenly a harsh voice behind the happy group said, "That's ours!"

Stunned, the three whirled about. In their excitement they had failed to hear Stilts and Umberto creeping up on them. Now the men stood over them menacingly, each brandishing a heavy stick.

"Thanks for leading us to the treasure!" Stilts said with a cruel smile.

CHAPTER 18

PINEAPPLE PRINCESS

"Don't you dare touch this box!" Señor Sifre cried out.

Stilts and Umberto advanced, nevertheless, their greedy eyes fixed on the emerald treasure. Umberto was nearest Señor Sifre. Suddenly the plantation owner sprang at him, grasping the stick before it had a chance to hit him. Their arms locked about each other. They tumbled to the ground, rolling over and over.

Meanwhile, Stilts came toward the two boys, swinging his stick menacingly. He just missed Pete's head. But quick as a flash Carlos grabbed the man's arm and Pete wrenched the stick from his grasp and threw it a distance away.

Stilts cried out angrily as he struggled to overcome the boys. But in a few moments they had him on the ground. Pete straddled his chest and held the man's arms while Carlos held his long thrashing legs until help came. Señor Sifre was having a hard battle but finally got his opponent down and got astride him.

"You will never take the treasure!" he shouted at him.

The panting fighters had not noticed the approach of the helicopter. But now they heard it and glanced upward. Ken hovered just above the spot and in a moment a policeman started down the ladder.

Stilts and Umberto made a desperate effort to get away but were held tightly. Another officer hurried from the helicopter and the two men were quickly taken in charge.

"Wait for me!" cried a voice above them and Holly came down the ladder, followed by Pam, Maya, and Ricky.

"We found the treasure!" Pete cried and quickly showed them the Infanta's crown.

All of them gazed in awe and exclaimed over its beauty. "It is worth a king's ransom," one of the policemen said.

"You mean an Infanta's ransom," Pam corrected him sweetly.

All this time Stilts and Umberto were glaring at the group. One of the officers said, "You have done the police a great service. We have been looking for these men. They are thieves who came from Florida only two weeks ago."

"It is very good that the Hollisters came to Puerto Rico," Señor Sifre said. "You have made everybody happy."

"Except these two thieves," Carlos said with a chuckle.

Quizzed by the two officers, the men confessed that they had heard of the Infanta's crown from

178

Pete wrenched the stick from his grasp.

treasure hunters they had met in Florida. In order to get to Puerto Rico they had stolen money on the mainland. They had been following the Hollister and Villamil children until they had uncovered the treasure.

"So it was you who listened under the window at Lizard Cove!" Pete said, pointing to Umberto.

The thief hung his head and confessed.

When Mr. Hollister had started out for Ponce, Stilts and Umberto had trailed him on motorcycles. "That's when Stilts discovered the secret of the second marker," Pam recalled.

The police quickly searched the two men and found a quantity of money in Stilts' wallet. "Was this what you got from selling Manuel's guitar?" Pete asked him.

At first the prisoner would not reply, but when advised that he had better tell the truth, Umberto confessed that this was true.

"Then we'll return it to the shop owner. He'll give it back to Mr. Targa," said one of the officers. "What will you do with the treasure?"

Pete said he thought the Infanta's crown should become the property of the Puerto Rican government and the others agreed.

"Let's put it in the museum at San Juan," Pam said, smiling.

After everyone had examined the ancient crown of the Spanish princess, Señor Sifre said, "Before you turn the crown over to the government, I should like to use it just once. I'd like to crown the pineapple princess of Puerto Rico with it."

As the others listened eagerly, the pineapple-plantation owner said he was holding a contest among visiting children for the honor of being named Export Pineapple Princess. With a wink at Maya, he added:

"We'll hold another contest for our local children and pick the pineapple queen."

The emerald crown was locked in a vault at police headquarters, but the chief understood that it was to be used to crown the pineapple princess.

During the next two days notices were put up in all the Puerto Rican hotels, and the San Juan radio and television stations broadcast news of the princess contest. It would be held at the Mar Caribe Hotel.

Sue, Holly, and Pam entered the contest. Nervously they dressed for it an hour before. The three girls wore long white dresses with gold sashes and bands around their heads.

As they were putting the final touches to their costumes before leaving for the hotel, Ricky popped his head into the room.

"Wouldn't I make a good pineapple princess?" he asked, his eyes sparkling impishly.

He pirouetted clumsily into the room. He wore one of Pam's fluffy white dresses and had tied a pink ribbon about his red head.

The girls roared with laughter.

"We'll make you the pickle princess," Pam giggled, "on account of all the spots on your nose."

"Don't make fun of my freckles," Ricky said, wrinkling his nose.

"We won't, if you take off my dress in a hurry," Pam said.

Ricky ran away and soon reappeared in a fresh tan linen suit. Then all the Hollisters and the Villamils left for the Mar Caribe Hotel.

The ballroom was crowded with youngsters, mostly from the mainland, who had entered the contest.

One by one the contestants, twenty little girls, paraded before a board of three judges. One was the editor of the local newspaper, another was a famous artist. The third was a New York actress in San Juan for a visit.

"Don't the little girls look lovely?" Mrs. Villamil said to Mrs. Hollister. "Your daughters are certainly adorable. Every one of them should get a prize!"

Mrs. Hollister smiled. "I doubt that they stand a chance," she said.

After the first parade of the girls, the field was narrowed to three children. The Hollisters beamed with pride as little Sue was named one of them.

The three girls paraded before the judges again. Sue walked straight ahead but her eyes darted from side to side and her dimples showed prettily. She curtsied before the judges. The other two remaining contestants were very pretty, but not as vivacious as Sue, whose brothers and sisters held their breath.

The three judges conferred a few minutes, then the actress announced:

"The Pineapple Princess is Sue Hollister!"

Everyone cheered and Señor Sifre, who had discreetly absented himself from the selection, stepped forth. In his hands he held the famous Infanta's emerald crown, but nestled in the center of it was the top of a tiny pineapple.

As Sue knelt on a red velvet cushion, Señor Sifre set the crown on her head. The little girl rose, her cheeks pink with excitement. Then she slipped her left hand into a pocket of her dress. As the onlookers chuckled, she pulled out her pet lizard. Holding the little creature close to her face she whispered:

"Lucky, you brought me luck!"

Quick as a wink, Lucky wriggled out of her hands and up onto the emerald crown. Then swishing his tail, the tiny iguana nestled in the pineapple.

"Just where we found him in the first place," Pam cried gleefully.